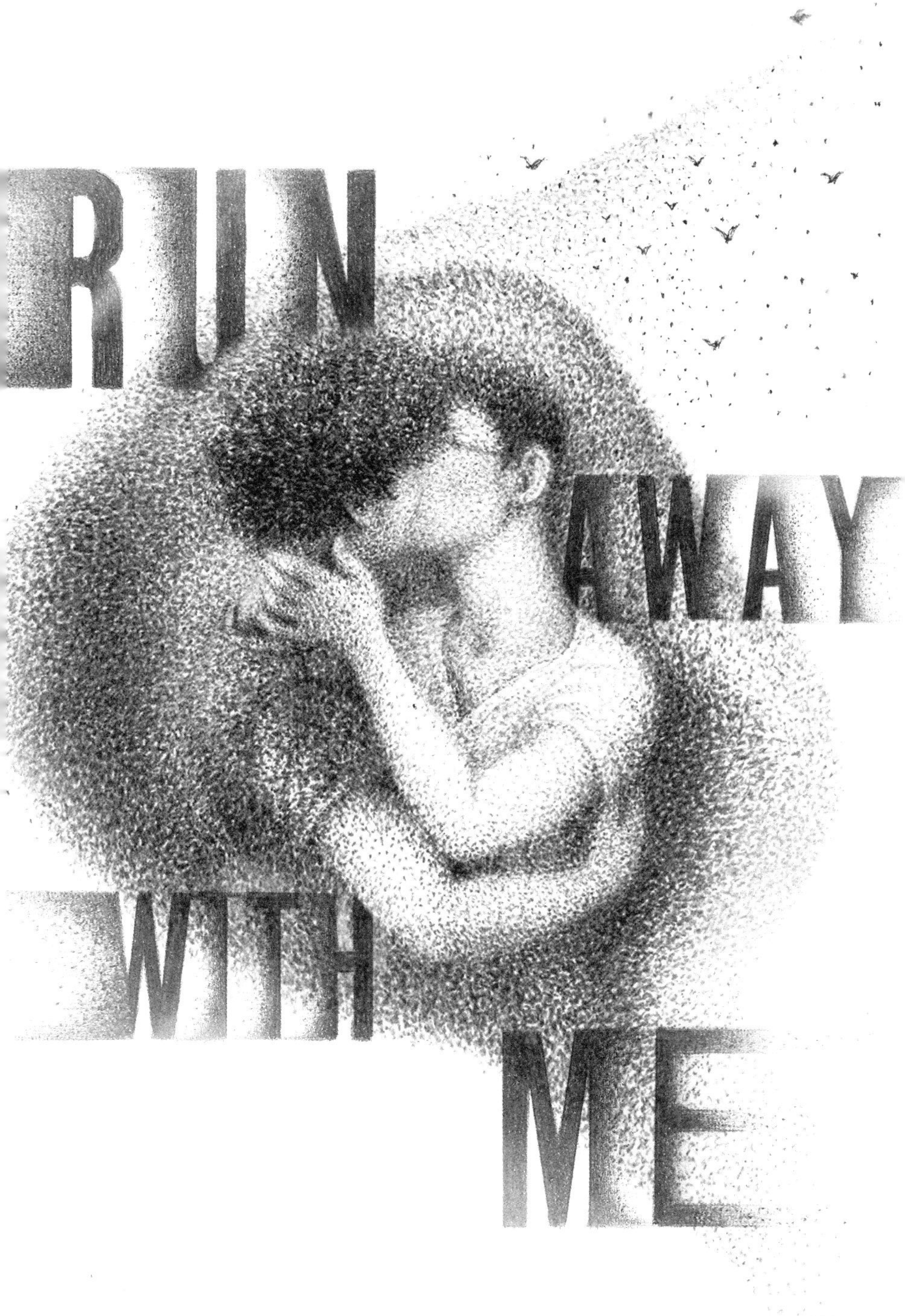
RUN
AWAY
WITH
ME

RUN AWAY WITH ME

BRIAN SELZNICK

Scholastic Press / New York

Library of Congress Cataloging-in-Publication Data available

ISBN 978-1-339-03552-9

10 9 8 7 6 5 4 3 2 1   25 26 27 28 29

Printed in China   127
First edition, April 2025

Book design by Maeve Norton

MIX
Paper | Supporting
responsible forestry
FSC® C144853
FSC
www.fsc.org

Per David Serlin
Ti Amo

Go thou to Rome—at once the Paradise,

The grave, the city, and the wilderness

  —Percy Bysshe Shelley, *Adonais: An Elegy*

    on the Death of John Keats, 1821

Everything I see advises and begs and forces

me to follow you . . .

    —Michelangelo Buonarroti,

     sometime after 1532

"Can I tell you a story?" Ilsa asks. Then

she adds: "I don't know the finish yet."

Rick says: "Well, go on, tell it. Maybe

one will come to you as you go along."

   —From an essay by Umberto Eco on

    Casablanca, 1985

PROLOGUE

Behind a huge wrought iron fence on the second-highest hill in Rome stands the Monda Museum, which isn't really a museum at all. There are displays and dioramas, but mostly it's the home of an organization dedicated to saving old books. This was where my mother and I were living for ten weeks during the summer of 1986. We had an apartment on the top floor with a balcony that overlooked the entire city. Arching over the balcony were three sycamore trees filled with wild green parrots that screamed during the day. The apartment was much nicer than the ones we usually stayed in, but there was only one bedroom, so I slept on a sofa in the living room under a window with no screens. It faced the back, where a giant umbrella pine stood across the street, silhouetted in the moonlight at night.

Silvio, the old security guard, told me the mysterious twin founders of the museum, Alberto and Vittorio Monda, had adopted for their personal use the two-faced god Janus, which was painted on their front door. The Monda brothers, who had never married, were supposed to haunt the place to this day. Silvio had not seen the dead men himself, he said, but he remembered one night many years earlier when he'd spotted a shadow in a window when he knew the museum was empty. He said books had been known to rearrange themselves when the moon was full, and sometimes words appeared in the dust, written by invisible fingers. I couldn't tell if he was making up these stories to scare me, or if they were real, but I never saw anything unusual myself.

No, the only thing haunting me that summer was a strange, curly-haired boy I met a few weeks after we arrived in Rome who told me he had no name and shared true stories that couldn't possibly have been true. He fed me fresh fruit and peeled back the layers of Rome, revealing to me foundations I never would have found myself. He took over my imagination until he was all I could see, in every brick and stone and sculpture of the city. He looked like an angel and declared, with great seriousness, that he was almost three thousand years old, having been on the brink of death for as long as anyone could remember.

I was sixteen when we found each other, shy and lonely and completely unprepared for what was to come.

He might have been a god, a liar, or both.

Either way, I made this book for him.

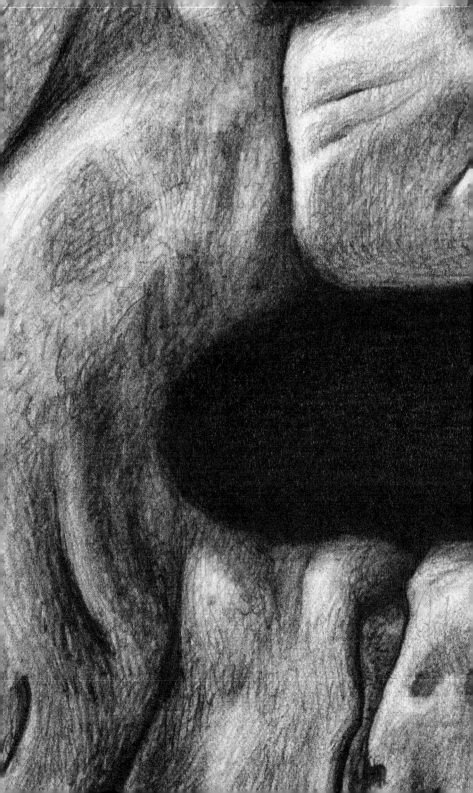

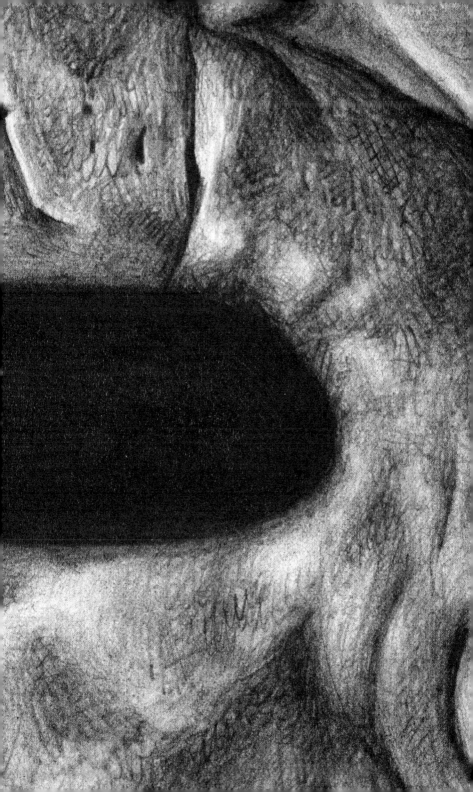

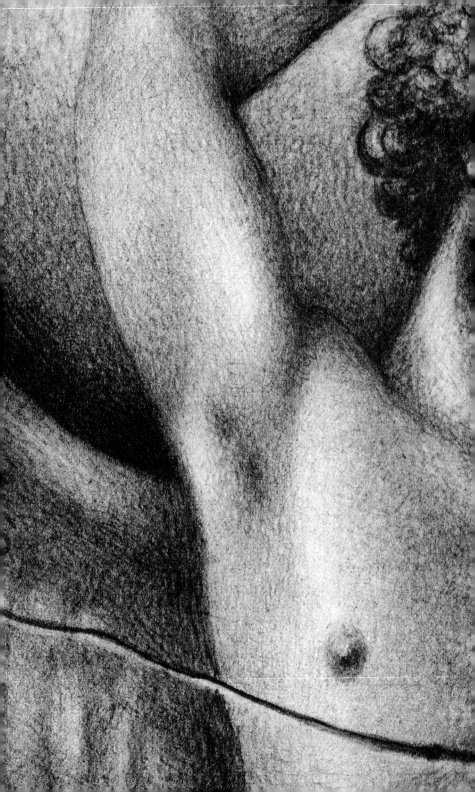

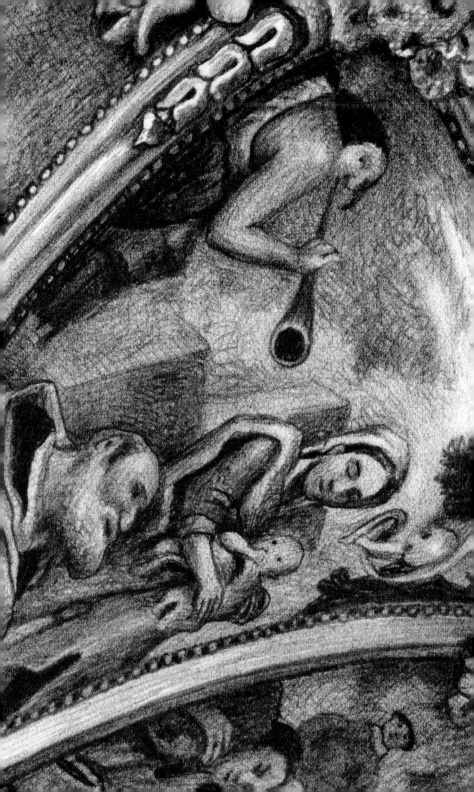

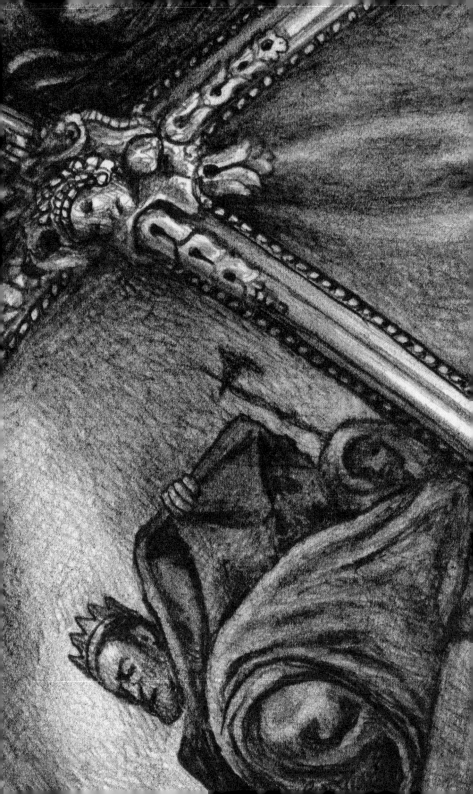

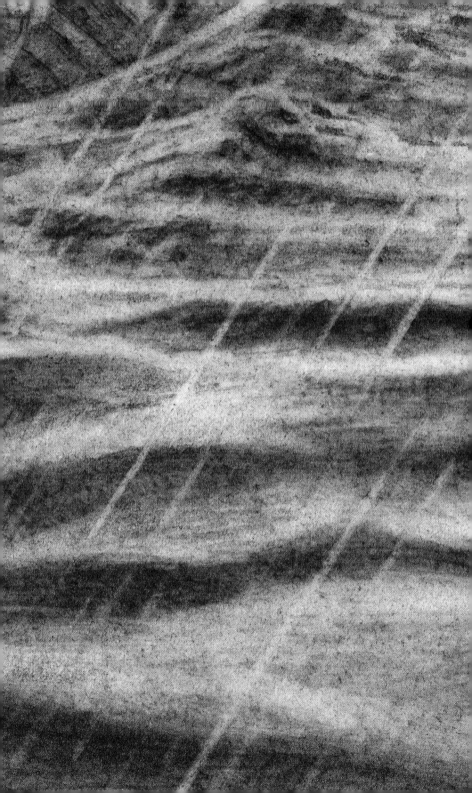

HEAT

I woke up in the empty church to the sound of rain. I thought I was still dreaming since it had been hot and sunny when I'd fallen asleep, but the weather must have seeped into my dreams, causing it to rain there as well. My clothes were damp with sweat.

I had gone to the Trevi Fountain a few hours earlier, where the heat had overwhelmed me. The crowd was taking photographs in the bright morning sun, throwing coins into the water and talking endlessly about the movies that had been filmed there. They pressed together so tightly it seemed as if our bodies would light on fire at any moment. I thought I might pass out.

At first it felt like there was nowhere to escape. But then I noticed two wooden doors at the top of a few steps across a small street to the left of the fountain. I'm not sure what drew me there exactly because there were lots of other buildings with wood doors within sight, but once I stepped inside, I knew the dark little church would be the perfect spot to rest.

I sat down for a moment on one of the wooden pews. But the church was so quiet, and the hazy light so calming, that I lay on my side, and slept until the rain made its way into my dreams and woke me.

Achy and uncertain of the time, I raised my arms and stretched. The noise of the rain pattered against the doors and windows. I straightened my glasses and looked up. Dull gray light was filtering in from above. It took a moment for my eyes to fully adjust, but there, lounging in a triangular area near the ceiling, was a life-size painting of an angel. He seemed to be staring at the other side of the room, and when I followed his gaze I saw another painted angel waiting above the opposite window, his arms resting over his head. Both were shirtless and beautiful, and there was something about the way their eyes met across the hazy space that fascinated and saddened me. Other angels could be seen wedged into tight corners around them, and an entire biblical story soared between them, but I found myself particularly intrigued by these two, with their wings folded uselessly behind them as if, at some point long ago, they'd forgotten they could fly.

Ever since we'd arrived in Rome, something odd had come over me, like the city was watching me and an invisible presence was following me, demanding I keep moving, though I didn't know what it was or where it wanted me to go. It was a very hard sensation to describe, like there was a clock ticking just over my shoulder or a mysterious engine was running beneath the ground, driving me toward some unknown destination. Whether I was eating dinner with my mother in the apartment after having bought the ingredients in shops where no one spoke English, or wandering alone through the ruins of the city, I felt restless. Even sitting in the church I had a sense I was supposed to keep moving. Usually what I wanted most was to find a place to take root, to be still. But it was as if all the molecules in my body were vibrating, and something deep and fundamental in my nature wanted to change.

I opened the door of the church, said goodbye to the angels, and plunged forward into the deluge, all the while thinking to myself, *What am I being driven toward?*

It was raining harder than anticipated, and I was quickly soaked through. The city dissolved around me into a vast maze of wet, hazy shapes seen through the spotted lenses of my glasses. I moved through the warm rain and the gray air, and the vibrations of my sneakers hitting the wet paving stones reverberated up my body.

I walked on, not knowing where or why, splashing up staircases and over misty bridges, down narrow side streets, under soaring umbrella pine trees that were too tall to actually keep anyone dry, and past endless, endless, endless ruins. I lost track of time and space in the rain. I started to wonder what it would be like if everything was washed away and I had no memory at all. No memory of my life, my mother, my vanishing schools, my temporary homes and missing friends. What would happen if I woke up and found myself alone with no past in this drowning city?

I walked by a tall gray shape that I knew was one of the thirteen obelisks of Rome. From our first days here, I had found myself drawn to the obelisks. My mother had walked me through the city with the same map she'd used eleven years earlier when we were living in Rome while she studied for a year at the Monda. I really didn't remember anything from when I was five, and she seemed a little disappointed. She kept telling me stories about how happy I'd been playing in the water of a fountain, or running through some ruins. But it was only when we came upon an obelisk that something would almost, just barely, seem familiar, as if there was an echo somewhere in my earliest memories. Yet I didn't share this with my mother. I wasn't sure why. She would have been so happy to know there was something real I might be remembering. Instead, I stared up at the towering stone objects, covered in unreadable symbols and hieroglyphics. They were so lonely and enigmatic, and my connection with them felt private somehow, as if no one else was supposed to know about it. Obelisks could be found all over Rome, and I imagined they marked the locations of events unknowable to me that had happened sometime in the deep past. Or, even better, maybe they indicated where something *would* happen one day in the unknowable future.

Most of the obelisks rose up from tall solid bases in the middle of open plazas, centered and strong, but a few looked like they were once owned by madmen who thought they could make the monoliths float midair. These were the ones I liked best. There was one in the Piazza Navona that hovered at the center of a huge fountain, supported by a kind of marble arch surrounded by four huge stone men, and there was one that balanced precariously on the back of a stone elephant in a plaza near the Pantheon.

As I continued on my walk now, I noticed that everyone had fled the rain, so it really did feel like I was the only person alive. There were no sounds except the endless whoosh of the downpour, and the only movements were the little flicker of a curtain in a shop window and the burst of a cat's tail on a ledge. Sometimes my eyes would play tricks on me, and I'd think I'd see a shadow pass by against a wall, but it was easy to imagine the entire world had been narrowed down to just me, the storm, and the paving stones.

Eventually I found myself at an intersection where a rain-slicked and broken sculpture sat high on a stone plinth. In our travels my mother and I had lived near a lot of art museums, and I'd grown to like statues very much. Unlike people, statues were always there, always the same, certain to never leave you. This particular statue, though, was startling to me. It had no face, no arms, no legs, and what was left of the torso was twisted into a nearly unrecognizable shape. It was rough, and wet. I'd passed by it a few times and it had always made me sad and uncomfortable. In a city filled with statues of triumphant gods and ancient heroes, I wondered why someone had put this broken thing on display. I was leaving the small plaza when, out of the emptiness of the endless rain, I heard a voice shout in English.

"Wait!"

It seemed as if the statue itself was calling to me.

An electric shiver rippled over my skin, and I found myself walking toward the broken thing. There were many notes written in Italian taped to the base of the sculpture or folded into various cracks. The rain had curled most of the paper, and ink ran down in rivulets. I tried to read what the notes said but couldn't. My mom spoke fluent Italian, and had tried to teach me before we'd left America, but I was basically illiterate in the language. Maybe this was part of why I had such an odd feeling as I walked around the city. When you can't read the words around you, it can make you feel foreign and invisible, and especially vulnerable.

I soon noticed there was one piece of paper, folded into a triangle, that was conspicuously drier than the rest. I plucked it from the stone, pressed myself against the wall to get away from the rain, and carefully unfolded it. Inside I found a hand-drawn map. I recognized the twists of the Tiber River that cut through the city like a giant's signature, the small island in the middle of it, the bridges that cross it, and the parks and main roads that surround it. What stood out, though, were thirteen small red marks that had been drawn across the map, and quickly I figured out they must indicate obelisks.

I looked around but still didn't see anyone. Who could have called for me and left the map? There were no words on it, no names and no dates, yet I had this odd feeling it must have been drawn just now, only for me.

One of the obelisks on the map was circled—the one on the back of the elephant. It wasn't very far, so I began walking toward it. What choice did I have? I needed to figure out what was going on.

By the time I got to the elephant obelisk I was aware of how heavy and uncomfortable my clothing and sneakers had become. I looked around, disappointed no one was there . . . until a shadow seemed to peel itself off a wall and move toward me through the rain. I wiped away the water drops on my glasses as best I could.

Standing directly in front of me was a boy about my age, his dark curly hair glistening with rain. He pulled me into the dryness of a nearby doorway, his fingers firm on the flesh of my arm. The touch startled me, but I instinctively followed. There was an urgency in the way he moved, and in the way he positioned me against the wall, his body near mine. He leaned close, and I could see he was slightly out of breath. One of his front teeth was chipped.

What's happening? I thought.

"They were built in pairs," he said, as if we were already in the middle of a conversation. "Did you know that?"

"What?" was all I could say. I was completely confused. Why was this stranger talking to me? Had he gotten me mixed up with someone else? I was so used to feeling invisible that I didn't understand how he'd seen me at all. It was as if his fingertips on my skin had set off a chemical reaction, transforming me into someone uncomfortably visible. I didn't know what to do.

"Obelisks," he replied. "In Egypt, they were always made in pairs." He had an accent, but his English turned out to be almost perfect. He pushed his wet black curls from his eyes as he continued. "They were only separated centuries later when people started stealing them to bring them here. So every obelisk you see, there's another one, somewhere, remembering it, waiting for it."

I couldn't help staring at him. It was like I'd imagined him into being, like he was one of the angels from the ceiling of the church made flesh, shorn of his wings and thrown down to the flooded Earth. "Was that you calling to me?" I asked. "At the broken statue?"

He shrugged.

"Was the map meant for me?"

"Yes," he said.

"Why?"

The boy shrugged again. "Who else would it be for?"

I had no idea what he could have meant by that. "But . . . what if someone else had found it first?" I asked.

"The statue wouldn't have given it to anyone else."

It was as if I'd found myself inside a myth, which should have worried me, as most myths didn't end very happily. People were usually transformed against their will into trees or constellations or deer killed by their own hounds.

I rubbed my eyes beneath my glasses and asked, "Have you been following me? I've been thinking someone was following me."

He didn't answer, but he smiled and we looked at each other. His eyes were dark, his lashes thick and curved. A long moment passed.

"Are you Italian?" I asked. His glare seemed to answer: *Don't ask stupid questions.* I looked up at the obelisk on the back of the elephant towering above us.

"They always seem lonely to me," I said. "The obelisks."

"They *are* lonely," he answered, as if the objects themselves had been telling him their secrets. "Even when they are riding an elephant."

"Carved by Bernini," I said, pleased I had remembered the name of the artist from my mother's map. I felt compelled to impress this boy.

"Bernini gets the credit," he replied, "because he was famous. But it was actually Dante Ferrata who did the work."

"Oh," I said. I should have felt a little deflated when he corrected me, but there was no judgment in the boy's voice, only pleasure. "Who's that?" I asked.

"Bernini's assistant."

"Oh."

"The obelisk was discovered in an excavation a few years earlier, and it was Bernini's idea to place it atop a sculpture of an elephant . . . but it was his assistant who carved the stone."

"I didn't know that," I said, half mesmerized.

He shrugged. "I know a lot of things. I've been here a long time."

"How long?"

"Two thousand seven hundred and thirty-eight years, two months, and seven days."

I laughed. What a weird thing to say. I found out later this was the exact age of the city of Rome on the day he and I met.

The rain stopped and we stepped out from the doorway. He reached his hand toward me and said, "I have so many things to show you."

"But . . . I don't understand. I don't know you."

"So?"

"So, what would you want to show me?"

"Everything. Come on."

"Wait. I don't even know your name."

"I have no name."

"What are you talking about? Everyone has a name."

"So give me one. Give me a name," he said.

"I can't give you a name."

"Then I'll give *you* a name."

"I already have one."

"Not one that matters," he said. Then he paused to think for a moment. He looked to the sky behind me where the clouds had parted, revealing a rainbow arching high above the elephant obelisk. He smiled, then said, "Danny. Your name is Danny."

"No it isn't."

"It is now."

"Danny?"

"Like Bernini's assistant. Dante."

"Dante," I repeated.

"But I'll call you *Danny*." He smiled slyly. "So, Danny . . . what are you going to name *me*?"

I took off my glasses and wiped them again. I knew I should just walk away. I'd learned my lesson about making new friends long ago, but there was something about this impossible boy that demanded my attention, and all I could think of was the church ceiling and the two angels with their curly hair and forgotten wings. I remembered how they had seemed to look at each other across the empty space, never able to actually move.

Before I could stop myself, I named him.

"Angelo," I said.

He looked at me with a dazzling kind of joy, deep and pure and full of surprise. I'd spent so long hiding in the shadows, looking longingly at others, I'd never imagined someone might want to look *back*.

The boy reached out his hand. My skin was cold and clammy and his palm felt hot against mine. I forgot about my waterlogged shoes and my dripping clothes. He wanted me to follow him, and at that moment I knew I would follow him anywhere, despite the inevitable separation and the worse loneliness to come. All that mattered right now was the shocking discovery of *us*—Danny and Angelo— Angelo and Danny—two names that felt right together, as natural as the rain.

We turned hand in hand and fell off the edge of the world, into the dark, wild abyss of Rome.

I moved through the city in a kind of daze. I felt newly born, as if I was a foal or an enchanted sculpture that had just emerged from a block of stone, and I didn't know who I was or what I was capable of. My life with my mother, the schools and cities and apartments where we'd lived, seemed to drift further and further away from me until everything was new, including the air I breathed and the legs I ran on. My skin felt as thin as tissue, and I barely understood where my body ended and the rest of the world began. So many new things were happening at once that it seemed like every time I blinked we were transported to another astonishing dream. I remember flashes of spires and bursts of windows, broken columns, undulating piles of cobblestones being repaved by workmen, and the smell of bread, jasmine, and coffee.

We ran inside the Pantheon and spun in circles around the tourists who stood beneath the glorious dome, where the bright white sky looked down on us through a perfectly round opening that reminded me of an unblinking eye.

"That's the oculus," Angelo said as he raced by me and a guard shouted for us, and in the next moment we were getting lost in the labyrinth of Rome's twisting cobblestone streets. I kept looking at this odd boy I'd named Angelo. His dark curls bounced in the air and his wet clothes clung tightly against his body. I caught his eyes, I saw them flash with mischief and pleasure, but I could only look for a moment before I broke our gaze. The intensity of his stare was too much for me. I'd look away toward the sky, or a statue, or the ground, but soon I'd be looking again at the turn of his calf, the way the blond hair on his legs shone in the sunlight, the arch of his back, the thin muscles of his arms. His neck was long and it made me think of a swan when he turned his head to tell me something about Rome. And then, because it felt like I had no other choice, I'd stare into his eyes until the shock threw me backward once again.

"You are visiting Rome, are you not, Danny?" asked Angelo as we walked down a road so narrow we touched the walls on either side with our outstretched hands. The rough stucco had fallen away in places and our fingertips traveled up and down across the exposed stones, climbing vines, and crumbling dust of the buildings around us.

"I am," I said.

"From where?"

Where was I visiting from? I guess I could have said "America," but that didn't feel quite right now, not after meeting Angelo. How could I describe it? My mother and I didn't live anywhere permanent. She worked with old books, so we usually found ourselves moving between universities with extensive libraries and various museums around the States. This meant there were always good schools to attend, but we almost never stayed longer than an academic year in any one place. We owned very few things other than my mom's personal book collection and her work tools, our clothes, and a few necessities like my tape recorder for music, which made it easier to move. We mostly relied on whatever our hosts had, or whatever was left behind in the apartments we rented from month to month. When I was very young, my mom and I lived near my grandmother in New Jersey so she could help take care of me while my mom finished graduate school in New York. She had come with us when we moved to Rome eleven years ago for my mom to study at the Monda, and she had died a year later. My mom sold the house and inherited some money, which helped with childcare, but her work was so specialized, she felt like she didn't have much choice but to follow whatever jobs she could get. That's why we started moving around a lot. I learned quickly that everything was temporary in my life. Other kids thought I was lucky because I saw so much of the country (and some of the world), and it really was interesting in many ways, but it was also tiring. During our travels I'd met military families whose kids dealt with something similar because their parents would have to move them from base to base around the world. There's no stability, no permanence, just an endless parade of new people and sudden goodbyes. Eventually there comes a point when you meet someone you might like, but you turn your back on them right away because you know the closer you get the harder it will be to leave.

I suppose I could have said all this to Angelo, but something stopped me. The reality of my life somehow seemed unimportant right now, or less interesting than the mystery of what this boy's story might be. Maybe I was scared too, afraid he might be uninterested, or disappointed in what I'd say. The thought of being rejected by him made an ache run through me that I worked hard to push away. Besides, I figured as we made our way down a narrow street, if he could say he was two thousand years old, then I could say whatever I wanted as well.

"I'm from outer space," I answered. "And I don't understand anything that's happening on this planet at all."

Angelo liked that answer. I could see it in his eyes. "How lucky you met me, then," he said. "I know everything."

"Everything?"

"Everything important."

"You know about obelisks."

"I do."

"And, Angelo?"

"Yes, Danny?"

I stopped beneath an open window. The sound of a radio hummed from inside. I realized I didn't know what I wanted to say. My mind went blank for a moment, then I answered with the only words I could think of: "I'm feeling very strange."

"So am I," he said, dashing ahead. I followed him, and we soon came upon a large open piazza filled with pigeons that took to sudden, ecstatic flight as we ran toward them. Our energy built and the two of us circled each other again, faster and faster until I grew dizzy and everything blurred except Angelo, whose chipped white tooth flashed before he ran off again, breathing hard, between two buildings on the far side of the piazza.

As we moved through the city, I allowed myself to hold his gaze longer and longer, until at last it felt as if I couldn't look away. It became a kind of game, where we'd see how far we could get from each other without seeming to blink, holding on to each other with our eyes. It was like a cord was binding us, lengthening and then pulling us back together, until we were touching again, breathing hard and laughing.

"We're a murmuration," he said as I stumbled toward him and his hands touched my shoulders to steady me. I was so distracted by the quick touch of his hands I didn't hear what he'd said, and asked him to say it again.

"A murmuration," he repeated.

"What's that?"

"It's what flocks of starlings do. Every winter the skies fill with starlings, and they fly in the most amazing patterns. It's like they're undulating and creating some kind of abstract black animation that keeps changing, like oil in water. Sometimes the vast shapes look like a single huge creature, or a giant ghost that fills the entire sky."

"Is that true?"

"It is. You'll see in the winter. A murmuration of starlings."

"A murmuration of starlings," I repeated, liking the sound of the words but knowing I wouldn't be here in the winter to see what a murmuration really looked like.

"And we are a murmuration of boys."

Angelo and I expanded and contracted across the city, a murmuration of two that shifted and changed shape but always felt complete and alive, no matter how big or small the space between us. He seemed to know every inch of the city. At one point, as we moved down a long, bending street lined with old shops, he stopped and looked into one of the display windows. The name of the store was painted in arched gold letters on the glass.

His profile was sharp and his lips were apart. He was breathing audibly. I came to stand beside him, to see what he was looking at. Inside the shop I could see a profusion of silver cups, marble statues, tumbled-up furniture, and stacks of Persian rugs. It looked like the whole street had shaken the contents of all its houses into this one space.

"Isn't it interesting?" said Angelo.

I assumed he was talking about the antiques, and nodded. "Yes, they are all very—"

"Not the things in the shop." He turned his face to me. "Us."

"Us?" I asked, as if I didn't know what the word meant.

"You from another planet, and me from another time. Isn't it interesting we've met?"

"Oh . . . yes."

"Will you tell me about your planet one day? I'd like to know."

"Really?"

"Really," he said, and for some reason I believed him, even though I didn't know a single true thing about him, not even his name. Whoever he was, I was thrilled he wanted to know more about me, and I began to wonder how I'd describe for him the lonely planet where I'd been living all my life.

We came upon a market in a large open square where Angelo purchased iced chunks of watermelon and a paper bag of cherries. We sat at the base of a large statue of a man in a long robe situated in the center of the square. Angelo told me the metal man towering over us had once been burned at the stake for telling the truth about the world. Gazing upward, I took a cherry and accidentally bit into the pit.

"Careful," said Angelo. "That's how I chipped my tooth."

"Watermelon's safer," I said, and we put our fingers around two red cubes. The fruit was shockingly cold in my mouth, and we spent some time trying to spit the seeds into a paper cup that had been discarded among a pile of leaves and stems by a nearby gutter.

At some point, the fruit sellers began packing up their unused crates and closing their large canvas umbrellas. I looked up and saw the sky had deepened in color, becoming more blue and orange and pink. The shadows had grown long and an army of brooms and overturned water buckets overtook the market, sweeping and splashing all around us.

"My mother's expecting me," said Angelo as a bee buzzed between the two of us. It was the first time he'd mentioned anything about his family, and it surprised me. "I'll walk you across the river," he said, "and up the hill to the Monda."

A flash of heat ran through me. I had never mentioned the Monda to him. I was sure of it, and for a moment I felt like the spinning world had stopped. "How do you know where I live?"

There was a little pause in Angelo's breathing, as if he'd gotten caught doing something wrong, but he recovered quickly and shrugged. "I've told you already. I know a lot of things."

I tried to read what I saw in his eyes. Something vulnerable had appeared, and his translucent pink eyelids quivered ever so slightly, like the wings of an insect aware of the imminent danger it faced. He'd been the leader and I had been following him, but now it felt as if I was the one in charge, the one who could save or destroy what we'd begun building that day. One wrong move would shatter the entire city and bring it tumbling down around us. So I said nothing, and we walked in careful silence over the Ponte Sisto bridge and through the bustling streets of Trastevere. We pulled ourselves up the long staircase built into the side of the hill and stopped for a cool drink in the basin of an ancient waterspout at the side of a road. Then we continued the steep ascent, until we came to a wide overlook at the edge of another huge fountain. We watched the sunset spread across Rome, and it looked as if King Midas had touched the entire world. Up the hill we went, until we arrived outside the gates of the Monda Museum. I didn't know what was going to happen next. I still felt afraid to speak, but then, in the purple twilight, Angelo's tongue touched the chip in his front tooth, and he said, "Meet me tomorrow at our elephant."

That was the phrase he used: *our elephant*. I liked that, and some-how the balance between us felt restored. Relief ran through me, knowing we were going to see each other again.

"I have a story to tell you," he added.

"Where do *you* live, Angelo?" I dared to ask.

"Nowhere. Everywhere."

"But . . . you said your mother is expecting you."

"I did?"

"Yes, you did."

"The starlings are my mother. The starlings, and the stars."

He smiled a mysterious smile, and ran down the street. Beneath an old streetlamp, he turned back to wave. Then he vanished around a corner, and our murmuration dissolved into the long, deep silence of the night.

"How was your day?" asked my mother.

"Fine."

I'd made up the couch with my pillow and blanket, and was lying down with my headphones, listening to The Smiths. She'd come in late from her office downstairs and was opening a few cabinets in the kitchen, which was only separated from the living room where I slept by a low counter with two blown-glass light fixtures hanging over it, one of which was broken. She wanted me to talk to her, but all I wanted was to have the room to myself. My entire body was pulsing with thoughts of Angelo.

"What did you do?" she asked as she rummaged quietly for something to eat. "Did you get caught in the rain?"

I felt like my mother would suddenly be able to guess all about Angelo if I uttered one more word, so all I said was, "No. Not really." I mean, what else could I have said? I turned over and faced the back of the couch, even though my mother would think I was being rude. The scratchy fabric smelled of dust with a hint of dampness, and straw.

"It was quite a downpour," she added quietly, as if she was talking to herself, and I could hear her pouring something, then I heard her walk over and close the huge shutters on either side of the doors to the balcony.

"Leave them open," I said. "I like the light in the morning."

I heard the shutters reopened.

I glanced up at the uneven wall across from me. The room was in deep blue shadows now, but during the day it looked like someone had been smoking here for two hundred years, staining everything a dark yellow. I could see the outlines of a few of the framed tourist posters and travel photographs that had been hung randomly on the walls, as if they were placed on nails that had been hammered in for other art, for other visitors, long ago.

My couch sagged in the middle, and I tried to adjust myself so my back wouldn't hurt in the morning. I didn't like any of the furniture in the apartment. It was all dark and heavy and completely mismatched, but my mom and I had rearranged everything when we'd arrived so the place would feel comfortable enough. This was something of a ritual every time we moved into one of our temporary homes.

When I'd returned after my day with Angelo, I'd been greeted by the combined scents of the old wood, fresh flowers (which my mother liked to buy every week), and decaying books. I'd been in a daze, barely aware of heating up the leftover soup from the fridge and toasting the last couple of slices of fresh bread. At some point I must have put on my headphones while I ate alone, with Angelo's black hair and wet clothes demanding my attention. And then I must have cleaned up, taken out my pillow, sheets, and blanket from the huge wooden sideboard, and laid them out on the couch

Now, as I listened to the sounds of my mother removing food from the fridge, I heard her say, "Nothing else to report?"

"No, not really," I said from the other side of the universe. "Sorry. I'm just tired."

I waited. I felt her looking at me, even though I had my back to her. *Please, just go*, I thought, amid my memories of ice-cold watermelon and Angelo's shining, chipped tooth.

"Sorry I had to work so late tonight," I heard my mom say. "We'll have dinner together tomorrow."

"It's fine," I said to the back of the sofa.

"Okay, then," came her voice. "Good night."

"Night." I wasn't sure if I said it out loud or only thought it.

I heard her turn off the lights and walk to her room with her dinner as her heels clicked against the marble floor. She closed the door, turned on her radio, and finally I was alone.

On my couch, beneath the window in our apartment at the top of the Monda Museum, I wondered for a moment if I'd imagined the whole adventure. But Angelo had to be real. His skin had been hot to the touch. In fact, lying here alone, I could *still* feel him, and smell him, all sweat and cherries and rain.

My heart pounded as if I was in the middle of a marathon. The only thing I wanted was to see him again, and I wished I didn't have to wait.

I pressed play and the song "Stretch Out and Wait" began. It's startling when songs you've heard a million times suddenly feel like they were written just for you, just for this moment—and that was what happened to me now. I felt tears on my cheeks and tasted salt on my lips as I listened, and stretched out, and waited. I stared up at the shape of the umbrella pine across the street; through my tears, and without my glasses, it hovered like an impossible island, a black rock suspended in the air. Trees may look like they are always standing still, but I'd read somewhere they just live in a different type of time than we do. If you filmed a tree over hundreds of years, then sped up the film, not only would you see it growing, but the bark on the trunk would be swirling and flowing just like water. Trees are in a constant state of movement, even if you can't see it. That's *me*, I thought. On the outside it may have looked like I was lying perfectly still on the couch, but on the inside I was writhing.

The cassette ended and I wiped my eyes. I slipped the player back under my couch as mosquitoes ceaselessly buzzed around me, biting me despite the orange-smelling spray I kept myself covered in. The wild parrots were quiet at night, but I heard a cat crying somewhere, and eventually, somehow, I slept.

In the middle of the night, a very loud sound, perhaps a book falling from a shelf, knocked me forcibly from my dream. I sat up with a start. At the edge of my mind, a memory from my dream hovered, then vanished.

My mother was still sleeping, and I began to wonder if the loud sound that had woken me up had been part of my dream. I looked around the blue shadows of the living room and it felt like something unseen was demanding I go explore the darkness. I slipped on a pair of shorts, put on my glasses, and went searching for a flashlight. The only thing I found was the small end of a candle in the kitchen, so I wrapped the bottom in tinfoil, lit what was left of the burnt black wick, and tiptoed past my mother's room. I quietly turned the lock on our front door, stepped through, and closed it again, testing it to make sure I wasn't locking myself out.

There was an ancient, dim lightbulb struggling to give off light from a battered sconce high on a wall at the other end of the hallway. Two other doors faced each other near the light, neither of which I'd ever seen open. I tried the knobs, but they remained tightly locked. The little flame in my hand flickered, and I knew I should turn back, but the feeling calling me forward was insistent, compelling me to walk downstairs into the empty museum.

Any building at night becomes a mysterious thing, but the Monda, with its darkened dioramas and scientific laboratories, was particularly uncanny by candlelight. At the front of the museum, the public area was divided into four large rooms. The first room, in honor of the museum's belief that books were living things, was a detailed exploration of how books are made called *The Birth of the Book*. Glass cases displayed antique printing presses and examples of binding techniques from all over the world, with jars of wheat flour paste and animal glue, binding frames, and piles of different-colored leather, paper, and board. The second room, *The History of the Book*, was about the ways stories and information have been shared through time, with a focus on libraries that went all the way back to ancient Mesopotamia. The third room, *The Death of the Book*, focused on how books can be destroyed. There were glass vitrines with examples of books that had been burned in fires, drowned in floods, shot in wars, stabbed in battles, eaten by insects, consumed by mold, faded by sunlight, and perhaps worst of all, books that had been cut up or blacked out with ink by censors. The final room, *The Resurrection of the Book*, was about the ways in which books can be saved. This was the real work of the Monda, and here you could see examples of the physical materials they employed and the scientific instruments they used. There were threads and binding tapes, more leathers, and a piece of kozo paper, which my mother used, and once allowed me to touch. The paper is so thin it seems to be spun from fog, and it can be applied to the back of damaged pages to help stabilize them and protect them from further deterioration.

The feeling in the air at night was hard to describe, like the entire building was holding its breath, or dreaming of tomorrow when people would return to bring it back to life. I'd walked by all of this many times already, but now the place seemed half-born, as if only I and my candle could reveal what was waiting in the shadows.

Behind the scenes, where the public was not allowed, the museum became even more fascinating. Large rooms with endless tubes and wires hanging from the ceilings were filled with moonlit glass beakers, jars of chemical solutions, piles of silver trays, and rows of stainless steel sinks. Dusty encyclopedias and damaged books waited everywhere for help, resting on shelves or wrapped in ace bandages like they'd sprained themselves. Behind a door with a sign that read CAUTION: RADIATION AREA, which my mother had told me never to open, were machines that probed and scanned books with something called beta-radiology, the way a doctor might x-ray your body for broken bones. As I walked through the museum I passed endless antique furniture with drawers and cabinets that contained scientific papers, catalogs, clippings, and who knows what else. My mother's lab was down a small corridor off one of these rooms, but I couldn't remember which one.

I wished Angelo was by my side. I wanted to see his face as I showed him everything, to feel his body next to mine. But, given the fact he seemed to know all of Rome, I wondered if he'd been here before, wandering the halls like I was doing. Did he love it already as much as I did?

I continued unseen through the halls, wondering if this was what ghosts felt like, trapped in the walls, unable to leave. Up until today, I'd been a sort of ghost myself, invisible and lost in the disintegrating city. But this morning I'd discovered miraculous things could happen here, like meeting a curly-haired boy who looked as if he'd fallen from the ceiling of a church, to remind me I was real, and alive.

A shimmer in the dark made me jump. It was Vee, the Monda Museum cat. His full name was Vittoriberto, named for the mysterious twin founders, Vittorio and Alberto, but everyone called him Vee. Silvio the security guard said the cat was famous all over Rome, and I had played with him when I was last here and he was just a kitten. According to the legend, when Alberto died and was buried beside his brother, a stray cat had wandered into the Monda through a window and never left. Someone came up with the combined name Vittoriberto, and every cat since then had been given the same name, so officially this cat was Vee the fourth, or fifth. I'd spotted Vee once or twice since I'd arrived, but all I'd usually see was his tail as he walked away from something or someone and vanished behind a piece of furniture. But for some reason on this night, Vee stopped when he saw me and jumped up onto an empty chair in the middle of the hallway and stared as if he really did recognize me. It was the first time I'd seen the cat's face. Candlelight glinted in his celadon eyes and there was something in his expression that made me think again of Angelo. I felt disoriented and displaced from time, like the border between dreams and waking life had dissolved.

Vee walked off as if he wanted me to follow him. He went down a long, dark staircase, tiptoed along the edge of a narrow hallway, then turned a corner and slid through an open door into a room I hadn't noticed before. Inside, boxes and books were piled everywhere. I saw rolled-up papers, stacks of broken shelves, and thick cobwebs hanging from the ceiling. Most of the rooms in the museum were immaculately clean, dusted and mopped several times a week by an army of blue-jacketed women with yellow pails, so the chaos was unexpected. I peeked into a few decaying cardboard boxes and found nothing but paper clips, nails, balls of twine, and old brochures about the museum, which I glanced at in the candlelight.

The Monda Museum and Book Conservancy began its life in the early part of the twentieth century as the private home of twin brothers Vittorio and Alberto Monda, eccentrics obsessed with books . . .

I skimmed through the text of the brochure and found myself intrigued by the two men. There was an old black-and-white photograph of them standing in front of the museum, though at the time it was their house. Behind them, painted on the door, was the two-faced profile of Janus. Vittorio and Alberto themselves looked like mirror images. Silvio the security guard had said the two unmarried brothers had kept many secrets, and I wondered what their lonely secrets might be. Together they cradled in their hands a small white object that I couldn't identify, though I noted how tenderly their hands touched each other.

I took one of the brochures, folded it in half, and put it in my pocket. I'd read the rest later.

Vee purred behind me, and I turned.

"What in the world . . ." I said out loud.

There, covering one entire wall of the room, which was about seven feet high and maybe ten feet long, was a vast antique map of Rome. It looked as if it had been pasted directly onto the wall many years earlier, as there were long rips and stains running down the paper. The sheer size and the intricate detail of the map almost overwhelmed me. My eyes traveled up and down the wall, and I traced my fingers across some of the roads of the city within my reach. Each road stood out in white against a darker background, crisscrossing one another and intersecting at open squares and piazzas. Even though the map seemed to be hundreds of years old, I recognized much of the city, because Rome, in many ways, hadn't changed very much. Every building, every obelisk, every fountain, every park and church, market, fortress, and lane where I'd walked since I'd arrived seemed to be on the map. I found the Pantheon; Piazza della Minerva, where the elephant obelisk resided; the Campo de' Fiori, where Angelo and I had bought fruit; and the long, curving Tiber River, which stretched from the floor all the way up to the ceiling. I could count four bridges spanning the water, including the Ponte Sisto, which was the bridge we had crossed that afternoon. I saw the little island in the middle of the river, which now floated just above my eye level, and the wide expanses, rolling hills, and farmland that would be claimed for Rome as the city expanded in the centuries after the map was drawn. At the bottom of the map, peeking out behind the dusty furniture of the room, was a decorative border with drawings of winged children, gods and goddesses, and the ruins of buildings that were already ancient when this map had been drawn, hundreds of years ago.

I must have taken all this in very quickly, because not long after discovering the map, I was startled by something brushing against the backs of my legs. I figured it was Vee, but when I turned to see if the cat was there, my little flame went out, and darkness consumed the city.

THE MOUTH OF TRUTH

"In Tunisia," said Angelo as we sat side by side in the shadow of the elephant obelisk the next day, "a child stood shivering on the bank of a river."

"Tunisia?" I asked. "Where's that?"

"The northern edge of Africa," answered Angelo before plunging back into his story. "Rain had started very suddenly, and the child had become separated from her mother in the darkness."

I wasn't sure why he was telling me this, but I was finding it very hard to concentrate because he had shifted his leg so our knees were touching. I pretended not to notice. It was very hot out and we were both sweating, even in the shade.

"The water was rising quickly," he continued. "The mud inched up her legs and she could feel the ground loosening beneath her and she knew she was going to fall. She cried out for her mother, but the wind and the rain and the river were too loud."

I tried to stay focused but I was too distracted by his skin. I found myself thinking about the storage room with the map I'd found last night. I knew I couldn't tell my mom or anyone at the Monda what I'd done, because sneaking around with a lit candle in an institution dedicated to saving books would probably get us kicked out, and even if—

"Danny," said Angelo, a note of worry in his voice. "Are you listening to my story?"

"I'm sorry," I said. "Yes, I'm listening."

"Good, this is important." He smiled and pressed his leg a little more firmly against mine. "So the storm was raging all around the child, and when the ground beneath her finally collapsed, she was swept away beneath the water so fast she didn't even have a moment to take a breath. Imagine how scared she must have been."

"Very scared," I whispered, happy to prove I was now listening.

"Just then, something long and powerful from beneath the water wrapped itself around her body, and she knew right away it was her mother's trunk. It lifted her up above the surface of the water and she was placed safely on the shore. She dug her four legs into the ground and reached out with her own much smaller trunk as the current grew too strong and her mother was swept away by the raging river—"

"Wait," I interrupted, finally moving my knee away from his so I could think. "The child is an *elephant*?"

"Yes."

I looked up. "Is it *this* elephant?"

"You'll see." He leaned forward so his face was very close to my ear. "The child already knew about death. An old elephant had died a few months after she'd been born, and like all elephants she remembered everything that had ever happened to her. The other elephants had wept and raised their trunks. They blew dust onto the dead elephant's body and covered him with leaves before the herd moved on. The child didn't understand what was happening exactly, but she knew it was very important to blow the dust and cover the body with leaves. Without doing that, spirits could not rest, and she knew she'd have to do that for her mother now."

"You're making this up, right?" I asked him quietly, because he was so close to me. I didn't want him to see that I was shaking slightly.

He shrugged.

"No one knows what an elephant is thinking," I added.

"Tell that to Dante Ferrata."

"Bernini's assistant? The sculptor?" I asked.

Angelo then smiled and jumped up. "Come on. Let's go back to the market."

We stopped in the Pantheon again to look up once more at the oculus in the dome, to see what the circular sky was like that day. Then, as we wandered up and down the shady stalls of the Campo de' Fiori, I asked more questions about my namesake, Dante, and the elephant. But Angelo wouldn't answer me. Instead we followed the rich smells of the endless mountains of spices, and the bright colors of the undulating stacks of ripe fruit. We bought more fruit, then ran down a short lane with the paper bags in our hands to Piazza Navona so we could cool off by the big fountain. Sitting beneath the four stone giants and the arch supporting the huge obelisk, we dipped the fruit in the clear water and ate greedily. The figs were rich and delicious, and the strawberries were so red and ripe and juicy, and the flavor was so intense, that I felt like I'd never actually eaten a strawberry before today.

A woman with dark hair walked by, and for a second I thought she was my mother. I must have jumped involuntarily because Angelo asked me if I was okay. I laughed in response, but my heart was racing. What did my mother think I was doing right now? I wondered. Reading at the apartment? Listening to music at a busy café by a fountain? Wandering alone through a museum, or buying bread using the few Italian words I'd memorized?

Whatever she thought, I knew it wasn't this.

There were lots of young men around us with their shirts off. I felt self-conscious sitting next to Angelo. He bit into a particularly large strawberry and bright red juice ran down his shirt.

"Oh no," I said, without really thinking. I reached my cupped hand into the water and leaned toward Angelo to wash off the juice before it stained, but he pushed my hand away with a force that surprised me.

"Don't touch my chest," he said. "You must never touch my chest." There was something in his voice like insecurity, or fear, though it was masked in anger.

"I'm sorry," I said, horrified and embarrassed by my actions. "I was just—"

He reached into the water himself, pulled the front of his shirt taut, and rubbed the long streak of red with his wet hands. His eyes caught mine for a second, and he seemed slightly embarrassed. Then he pointed at something behind me.

"Look," he said.

"What?"

"That man," he answered. "The one with a beard."

I looked around but saw no one with a beard.

"He looks just like the Mouth of Truth," said Angelo. "Doesn't he?"

"The what?" I asked.

"The Mouth of Truth! You do not know what that is?"

"No."

"Oh, good. It is another thing I will show you."

Angelo rose and beckoned me to come with him. For a moment I tried to figure out how I could ask him about his chest, about what had just happened with the water, but I couldn't find the right words. Maybe it was because we barely knew each other, but I was afraid of breaking whatever was starting to connect us. So I took a deep breath and off we went in silence. He led me down narrow, crooked streets, and helped me over ancient stone walls, becoming my guide once again.

We came to Largo di Torre Argentina, an excavation site the size of an entire city block surrounded by roads and tram lines that converged from all over Rome. You could look down from the edge of the streets into a large area filled with the exposed ruins of temples and Roman theaters. A semicircle of broken, uneven columns rose into the air, and the lowest parts of many stone walls created a kind of three-dimensional blueprint of the buildings that had stood here long ago. Mountains of carved marble pieces and rubble lay everywhere, as if waiting patiently for archaeologists to put them all back together. I'd passed this area a few times previously but hadn't really stopped to look. Now, though, I was very aware of the jagged surface of the excavation, and how it stood in stark contrast to the order of the surrounding streets and sand-colored buildings.

"It's like the city is having surgery," said Angelo quietly as we walked along the length of the excavation. "Cut open to let you see inside."

"There are so many cats," I said, having noticed what looked like hundreds of them living among the ruins and passing among the legs of the people walking by on the sidewalks above.

"They've been here forever, living like royalty," he said. "People bring them food and water, but they exist in their own society. They have their own affairs, their own families and secrets. It is illegal to harm them. Even the government knows to treat them like gods. You should have seen how worried everyone was last winter."

"Why?"

"It almost never snows in Rome, but there was a big storm last winter with icy winds that came all the way here from Siberia. The whole city shut down. We had snowball fights and built snowmen, and when I walked here, I saw crowds of people bringing bowls of food and thermoses full of warm milk for the freezing cats. For Romans, snow is unusual and miraculous."

"Miraculous?"

"Once, there was a pope who dreamed it snowed in August, and the snow fell in the shape of a church. When he awoke, he commanded the church be built. It was considered a miracle. Don't you believe in miracles?"

I didn't know how to answer him. I think the closest I'd ever come to experiencing a miracle was right now, but that was another thing I couldn't say. So I stayed quiet.

"Come," he said. "The Mouth of Truth awaits."

We moved on from the kingdom of the cats and continued through the city until he pointed to an ancient temple and an old church at the top of a long road.

"That's where Romulus and Remus were rescued as babies."

"The founders of Rome?" I asked. I'd read about them somewhere.

"Yes, they were abandoned to die at the edge of the river. They were saved by a wolf. Romulus eventually killed Remus to become king of the city. Rome is founded on murder."

"Oh."

"Well, imaginary murder. It's a myth. But isn't it interesting we made up a story about death to explain ourselves? Maybe we need to explain the sense of danger that always hovers in the air."

"Is there a sense of danger in the air?"

"You haven't noticed? Always. They used to call it Roman fever. There were so many stories of people going out for walks at night to damp places like these ruins, which were once overrun with grass and trees. They'd meet someone they shouldn't have met, or stay out too late, and the next thing you'd know, they'd be dead."

"Oh," I said again, feeling a little worried. My skin burned and I wondered if I had Roman fever. I think Angelo saw the look on my face as I wiped my forehead.

"There is no more Roman fever," he assured me. "It turned out to be malaria, which is gone from here, though other threats remain. But that's what we do, right? Navigate through the danger. Otherwise we would never leave our houses, and that's not safe either because most accidents occur at home." Angelo shook his head as if to clear his thoughts. "Enough of that. Onward."

At the top of the road, he took me to an open gate in the front of the church. It led into a pink portico that housed a huge, bearded face carved on a stone circle that sat on a small pillar against one of the walls. The face was flat and there were long cracks through the hair and beard. The face's eyes, nostrils, and open mouth were carved all the way through, as if it were the mask of a giant.

"This is it. *La Bocca della Verità*. The Mouth of Truth. He is a god of the sea. But that is not why I brought you here. I brought you here because he eats liars."

"He *what?*"

"Well, their hands, at least according to the legend. You put your hand inside the mouth. If you are a liar, he will bite it off. But if you are not, no problem. I will show you." He then plunged his hand into the mouth, and immediately his eyes went wide as he tried to remove it again but couldn't. My heart leapt and I reached out to help him; he quickly pulled his hand from the mouth and laughed. "It is a joke from a movie called *Roman Holiday*," he said. "But everyone does it. My hand is fine. See? I am not a liar. Now go on, put your hand inside, so I can see if *you* lie."

I hesitated briefly, then put my hand into the stone mouth.

I wasn't sure if I imagined it, but the air I touched on the other side of the face was cooler, and somehow it felt . . . dark. I knew this was a god of the sea, but the god I thought of was Janus, who had two faces and presided over beginnings, transitions, and doorways. This mouth was a kind of beginning, a type of transition, a sort of doorway, and I was now on two sides at once. I thought about how people always wanted me to choose one thing. Adults were always asking, *What are you going to be when you grow up?* as if there's only one thing you can choose. Why was it so uncomfortable for people to think about being many things at once?

I pulled out my hand and looked at Angelo, stretching my fingers and rolling my wrists. "I'm not a liar," I said. "It didn't bite me."

"Not today," he answered with a smile.

No one was around. We stood there, in front of the huge stone face, and neither of us said a word. Somehow the weight of the silence felt powerful and full of meaning. It was hot, even in the shade of the porch, and I thought again about Roman fever. I knew I didn't have malaria, but something else was making me burn.

"Do you like the Mouth of Truth?" asked Angelo.

I looked at his lips, which were still red from the strawberries, and I said, "Yes. I like it very much."

Somehow the entire day passed. We walked and wandered, talking sometimes, and other times just letting the beauty of the city carry us in silence. We ate olives and cheese and sandwiches Angelo bought from tiny shops, and we sipped water from gurgling old fountains with curving nozzles at the sides of the streets. He told me they were called *nasoni*, which meant "big noses," and showed me that if you stop up the water falling from the end of the nozzle with your finger, it shoots out a small hole at the top, creating an arc from which you can more easily drink, like a water fountain at school. We climbed up and ran back down a staircase called the Spanish Steps, at the top of which was an obelisk, and at the bottom of which was a funny little fountain Angelo said was called the Fountain of the Broken Boat. People gathered all around it, drinking from the four spouts pouring from its sides, as if the stone boat had sprung massive leaks.

Before we knew it, the sun started to set, and we found ourselves halfway across the city, walking past the giant round ruins of the Colosseum. Angelo had no interest in going inside. "It's too crowded," he said. "And it was built mostly for death. No, I have a better idea."

We ran down a street called Via Labicana, and I followed Angelo into a three-sided courtyard.

"Welcome to San Clemente," said Angelo. "It's medieval, built around 1100."

The building was closed to visitors, but he knew where to squeeze through a metal gate. We tiptoed into the dark sanctuary, and back by the altar he pushed open a small door I wouldn't have otherwise noticed. We descended a staircase, and after what seemed like a thousand stone steps we came to an open floor lit by dim safety lights that must never turn off. The deeper we moved, the cooler and damper the air became. There were broken columns and remnants of mosaics still decorating the walls.

"Now we're in a Byzantine crypt," Angelo explained. "From the year 400."

He found another staircase and down we went, continuing step by step back through time until he led me to a small room with a stone table in the middle.

"This is where people used to worship gods whose names we no longer know," he said. "All of Rome in one way or another is like this. Layers of history, built one on top of the other."

I could hear water flowing somewhere, which surprised me, given how deep underground we were. Angelo took my hand again and we walked through a narrow, curving series of arched stone hallways until we came to a small room where the sound of the water grew very loud, enveloping us beneath a rounded concrete ceiling. The walls were made of ancient bricks, stacked in various patterns. It felt like the room was quietly protecting us.

"Somewhere behind these walls," he said, "is a house that dates to the time of Emperor Nero, which was destroyed in the great fire of Rome in 64 BC. We've just traveled back almost two thousand years." He paused so the sound of the water filled my ears again. "But we can go back even further," he said as he pointed to the corner, where I found a rectangular opening in the floor. "Be careful," he said as I leaned over. Rushing directly below us was a river.

"Touch it," he said, and I lowered my hand. The water was cold and clean.

"I've always thought it's like touching time itself," Angelo said. We both cupped our hands and scooped some up to drink. It was as crisp as a winter lake and as refreshing. Once I swallowed I actually said "Ahh!" out loud and immediately scooped up more.

"This is the reason Rome pulses with life and history," continued Angelo after he wiped his mouth with the back of his hand. "This water has been running nonstop beneath the city for all of eternity. It's the source of every fountain and aqueduct you see across the city. This same sound has been filling these walls forever."

I looked at the water and wondered what it was running toward.

"Do you visit this place a lot?" I asked.

"This is where I live," he answered.

"No, it's not," I said, and suddenly I felt lost. What was I doing down here, beneath the earth with a boy I didn't know? I had a thousand questions I wanted to ask him, like *Why do you say such strange things?* and *What kind of game are you playing?* and *Where do you really live? What do your parents do? Do you have brothers or sisters? Where is your school?* But all I could manage to say was, "You haven't told me anything about yourself."

"I've told you many things about myself."

Nothing real, I thought.

"Take me back to the Mouth of Truth," he said quietly, "and ask me where I live. Is that what you would like to do?"

"But . . . there's no furniture here, no books, no food. It's just empty stone rooms. You can't live here."

For what seemed like a very long time, the only sound was the water running endlessly beneath us.

"What about you?" he said. "You told me you were from another planet."

"I don't live anywhere," I answered. "Not really."

"Now I am the one who wants to bring you to the Mouth of Truth."

"What I mean is, I'm always living *somewhere*. It just hasn't been the same place for a long time. It's been a while since I've gone to the same school in the same state two years in a row, or slept in a bed that really, truly felt like my own, or stayed in a room that fully belonged to me."

"What about your friends?"

"I have no friends."

"That can't be true," Angelo said. "Come, let's walk around before it gets dark."

As he led me back upstairs, forward through time, I said, "I've *had* friends."

"Ah," he said as we climbed.

I wasn't quite sure why I suddenly felt like I had to prove something to him. I said, "Stevie was the first friend I remember. He loved playing with Legos. And Jenny never wore shoes, and Jonathan taught me how to play chess." We continued upward, and I spoke quietly to Angelo's back. "I always cried when I had to leave at the end of the school year, and each time it happened I felt worse, and I got more angry at my mother for making us move all the time. Then when I was thirteen I met a boy in San Diego named Adam. His parents were in the military, and he became the best friend I'd ever had. We had most classes together, but when we were apart all I could think of was hearing what he'd been up to and sharing with him what he'd missed. I was dreading the end of the year, when my mother was going to make me leave, but one night his parents took *him* away. They didn't let him say goodbye. It was like I woke up one morning to find he'd just vanished from the face of the earth."

Here's what I *didn't* say: that from the moment I met Adam, we clung to each other, arm in arm, legs intertwined. Sitting together at lunch and during assemblies, we'd find ourselves leaning against each other without even realizing it, fingers digging into skin and denim. I thought I wasn't going to survive when he was taken away because it hurt so much. A black hole had opened up, and I couldn't stop crying. That's when I'd made the decision to keep to myself as much as possible. If I stayed by myself, there would be fewer people to grieve for. And even though Adam left before I did, I'd decided I'd never forgive my mother. After all, I rationalized, we lived like this because of her.

At the top of the last staircase Angelo turned to me. There was something odd in his expression, something it took me a moment to figure out. Finally I realized: He *understood* me, really deeply understood what I was telling him. And there was such profound sympathy in his eyes that suddenly I did not know what to do. No one had ever looked at me like that. Well, maybe Adam and I had shared something similar, but we were younger, and everything seemed less fraught back then, less dangerous.

"Lucky you," said Angelo.

This was about the last thing I expected Angelo to say. Nothing in what I'd told him made me feel lucky. I said nothing, but Angelo must have understood the expression on my face because he answered what I hadn't asked.

"To have had a friend," he said. "Even for a short time. That's important."

He and I emerged into the modern era beneath the darkening sky. As we reentered the golden city, he said, "Why are you living at the Monda?"

"My mom is working there for the summer."

"Just the summer?"

"We leave August fifth."

Saying the date out loud for the first time caused something distantly upsetting to settle between me and Angelo, like I'd just lit the long fuse of a bomb.

Neither of us said anything for a while as we moved through Rome, eventually coming upon more dusty antique shops that lined one side of a plaza. We looked through the glass windows at the Aladdin's cave of objects for sale: gold chairs, miniature obelisks, mosaics wrested from some ancient home, marble copies of famous statues, and eighteenth-century paintings of the Colosseum when it was covered in trees and grass.

As we walked from shop to shop, I believed Angelo and I were thinking the same thought about not being together, that we had become aware our time, like with all my other friends, was limited.

We eventually found ourselves beneath the dome of the Pantheon again, and looked up at the vision of the purple sky cut into the oculus above us. Angelo asked, "What about your father?"

"He's not in our life," I said. "And my mom doesn't like to talk about him much. She got pregnant with me in grad school. He was also a student. I don't think I was something she planned on."

"I also have no father," said Angelo quietly.

"What happened?" I asked, but Angelo shook his head, indicating he didn't want to talk about it.

"Life is full of surprises," he said. "Good ones and bad ones."

"Which am I?" I asked, almost without thinking.

"I don't know yet," he answered with a quiet laugh as we walked out of the ancient building, through its massive iron doors. People had come out for their evening stroll, which Angelo said was called the *passeggiata*, and everywhere the streets and sidewalks and piazzas were filled with chattering couples, slow-moving old people, and packs of loud teenagers spreading and contracting around everyone else with bursts of noise and music. And through it all, Angelo and I floated together.

"What is your mother's job at the Monda?" he asked me.

"She's a librarian, and a historian, and a book conservator."

"That's a lot of things."

"Her specialty is old manuscripts, and paleography."

"Paleography? What's that?"

I liked knowing something Angelo didn't. "Like when handwriting is hard to read. She can figure it out. She's really good at it. She studied paleography at the Monda for a semester in graduate school, eleven years ago. They invited her back this summer as part of a grant the museum received from the Italian government to study an old book they unearthed recently. One of her teachers remembered her, and thought she'd be the best person to work on it. Or something like that."

"So you've lived in Rome before."

"I don't really remember much. I was five. The old security guard at the front gate says he remembers me and my grandmother playing in the garden while my mom studied. He can't stop talking about how tall I've grown."

"You have an interesting life," Angelo observed.

I shrugged. "I don't know. It's just my life."

"Did you ever notice that everyone thinks their own life is normal, but each person's life is so *different*?"

"I suppose."

"So what is normal, really? I'd say nothing. Nothing is normal."

We stopped to get gelato from a silver cart run by an old man in a baggy yellow shirt. With the sweet coldness dripping over our hands, we ran down a long stone staircase to the edge of the river, and pretended we were hacking our way through the overgrown vines under the embankment.

"The book," said Angelo, licking the last of his red cherry gelato from his fingertips, "the one your mother is working on. What is it about?"

"I don't know. It was found behind a hidden panel in the house, I think."

"Hidden? That's interesting."

"They think it's rare, and might be valuable, which is why they got the grant, I guess. The handwriting is so illegible, they think it could be a code, but either way it needs to be deciphered. Mom believes it might be a collection of poems."

"Poems?"

"Love poems, maybe," I said, and Angelo smiled. It seemed like he'd finally gotten the answer he'd been waiting for.

"I've told you already. *Nothing* is not an answer."

I took a breath and rearranged the silverware on the table as I tried to figure out a way to edit Angelo out of my day. There were so many reasons to keep him secret, and right then, navigating the little kitchen area in our apartment as Mom cooked, I couldn't help believing that if no one knew about Angelo, I could somehow stay with him forever.

"I mostly just walked around," I said. "I got some fruit from the market."

"Campo de' Fiori?" asked my mom.

"Yeah, I think so. By the huge plaza with the fountain."

"That describes half of Rome."

I laughed.

"Did you bring anything home for us?" she asked. "I meant to ask you to get something for dessert."

"Oh, sorry. No."

"Next time," she said as she shaped the pasta dough she'd made. My mother was a pretty good cook, and she liked making something that she called *pasta brutta*, or "ugly pasta," which was hand rolled and uneven. A simple sauce of garlic, tomatoes, and olive oil was simmering on the stove behind her, next to a huge vat of water that was about to boil.

"Smells good," I said. She was concentrating on rolling the pasta and didn't answer. "Mom?" I said a little louder. She looked up. Thinking still of Angelo, I asked, "How is the book? Did you figure out any of the poems?"

She smiled a little. "Not today," she said as she threw two handfuls of salt into the now-boiling water and tasted it with a wooden spoon. When the water was salty enough, she dropped in the twisted spikes of pasta, and just a few minutes later everything was done. I plated the bread and got the butter from the counter, where it stayed in a glass dish, soft and warm. We sat and my mom took a sip from her glass of wine. "So, seriously," she said, "I want to know what else you did today."

I sighed.

"Don't sigh," Mom said. "It's rude."

"I didn't sigh."

She glared at me as we chewed. I had to answer with something, so I told her, "I saw the Mouth of Truth."

"You did? How did you find that? Did you read about it, or have you seen *Roman Holiday*?"

I shrugged, regretting my decision to mention it. "I guess I read about it."

"Did you put your hand into the mouth?"

I could have said yes, because it was true, but saying yes felt too closely linked to my thoughts about Angelo, so I shook my head. As the silence grew, I had a feeling my mom knew the giant stone face would bite my hand completely off if we were there, and I shivered.

We finished the meal in silence.

THE MONDA BROTHERS

Late the next morning, Angelo and I were eating sweet pastries and drinking espresso at a little round table on a street not much wider than the cars that slowly passed us by. I'd never really liked coffee, but Angelo told me I needed to learn to appreciate the bitter intensity, so I tried. I found myself thinking about the brochure I'd taken from the secret room, and with our espresso cups shining near us in the sun, I pulled it from my pocket and opened the folded paper. I showed Angelo the photograph of the brothers, and the mysterious white object held gently between them.

"I know this brochure," he said.

"You do?"

"My mother has one from a long time ago."

"She does?"

I could feel the edge of Angelo's foot move to the edge of mine beneath the table. He shrugged as our hands took opposite sides of the brochure, holding it open, and our shoulders and elbows touched, gently binding us. Soon, even our breathing synced up. Together, we read the brochure.

The Monda Museum and Book Conservancy began its life in the early part of the twentieth century as the private home of twin brothers Vittorio and Alberto Monda, eccentrics obsessed with books. They'd arrived in Rome as young men, leaving no trace of their origins. They purchased a crumbling seventeenth-century palazzo at the top of the Janiculum Hill and, over time, were said to have collected over seventy million books. Rumors spread that the Mondas maintained an impossible underground library larger than all of Vatican City.

Vittorio and Alberto adopted as their personal logo the double profile of Janus, the god of beginnings, transitions, and doorways. The Janiculum Hill was named after this god, and could be the simple reason they chose him for their personal use. But perhaps the real reason they adopted Janus, and not the twin founders of Rome, Romulus and Remus, for instance, was because they thought books—like Janus— could see into both the past and the future.

Alberto was said to love puzzles, and no one was ever able to figure out the exact system he put in place to organize their collections, so its details are shrouded in mystery. One thing, however, is clear: The brothers were most openly passionate about works by John Keats. The young English poet had died over a century earlier in a small bedroom beside the Spanish Steps in Rome. Supposedly, the Monda home had seven hundred feet of shelf space (about the length of an entire city block) devoted to Keats and his poetry.

Vittorio died, possibly of a heart attack, in 1946, and afterward Alberto shut the house completely. Twenty years passed and almost everyone forgot about the brothers . . . until a massive flood devastated the city of Florence, threatening tens of thousands of books, many of them irreplaceable. No one knew what to do, but the next morning telegrams arrived at the offices of all the rescue agencies in Italy. To everyone's shock, the telegrams had been sent by Alberto Monda, announcing he would spearhead the effort to save the city's drowned books. Having been unable to save his beloved brother, it turned out Alberto had spent the previous twenty years learning how to save books. He pioneered endless new techniques, including the radical idea of freezing waterlogged books to keep them from rotting. Because of his efforts, most of these rare books were saved.

After Alberto's death, the Monda House was taken over by the city of Rome, and quickly became the central institution for books from around the world that needed to be rescued and repaired. Today, the small but dedicated staff continues the brothers' legacy, collaborating internationally with libraries, museums, and laboratories in an unending effort to help any book whose life is in serious danger.

Neither of us spoke for a little while, but it felt like the stories we'd just read hovered between us, like the air was filled with books.

"Your mother must be very special," said Angelo eventually, "to work in such a place. To be an expert the experts turn to. Not many people do such an important thing."

What could I say to that? Except for *expert,* none of these words were words I'd ever associated with my mother. I'd never thought of her as *special* or the work she did as *important.* How interesting to see my life reflected back through the prism of Angelo. Everything seemed bigger, and more wonderful, and I had no way to express any of this to him, except perhaps to smile, which I think I was doing, because he smiled back.

I found myself thinking about Vittorio and Alberto, who I could imagine very clearly, walking together among their endless shelves. I tried to imagine Alberto's grief when Vittorio died. It all felt so real to me, and present tense. As present tense as my mother, bent over her desk in her office, with a magnifying loupe to her eye, working to decipher a revelation from swooping, indecipherable ink.

"Do you want to meet them?"

It was Angelo's voice, of course, but I was confused. "Meet who?"

"Vittorio and Alberto."

"The *Monda brothers*?"

"Yes."

I laughed, or I made some kind of sound that I couldn't control. "They're dead," I pointed out.

"What does that matter?" Angelo answered casually, finishing the last drops of his coffee, and spinning a silver coin from the change he was leaving on the table.

A boy's face was staring at us from behind the dirty window of a closed newspaper shop. Given the rusty chains and dirty glass, the place seemed to have been shut for many months. Perhaps the owner had died suddenly, I didn't know, but it was like a little time capsule had accidentally been created when the store was locked up. Angelo and I were near the entrance to a park at the top of the Janiculum Hill when the boy's face on the front page of an old newspaper caught my eye through the glass. He had a sweet expression, but sad eyes, which were still clear despite the fading yellow paper. I couldn't read the headline.

"Do you know who that is?" he asked me.

"No," I said.

"An American boy. He was in all the papers."

"Why? What did he do?" I could tell the answer wasn't going to be a good one.

"He had AIDS, from a blood transfusion, and was told he could no longer go to school. He came to Rome for a visit. He even went on television. There were stories about him everywhere."

"Oh," I said. "Did he die?"

"I don't know."

Angelo led me forward. "Come, I want to show you something before we meet the Mondas."

We entered the park and walked past fields and lakes and fountains and little gardens with crumbling statuary to a grove of umbrella pines. I had always liked looking at the one outside my window, but there must have been hundreds of them here, lined up in long perfect rows, creating a huge grid. It felt like a cathedral of trees when you stepped beneath them.

"I love this place," Angelo said. "A famous musician once wrote a piece of music about it. I'll play it for you sometime."

We found a spot in the middle of the grove, lay on our backs in the grass, and gazed up at the canopy. There was a hush in the air, like we were in the middle of the woods, yet whoever had planted these trees long ago had taken away all the disorder and chance associated with a wild forest. No wonder a musician had written music inspired by this place. Lying here with Angelo was like being *inside* music, though the music was something you felt, not something you really heard.

For a long time we stayed on our backs, just looking up. The intensity I felt being near him was still very present, but there was something new creeping in at the edges, something I couldn't quite identify, which was bothering me. Maybe it had to do with the sick American boy, or maybe the lingering danger in the city that Angelo mentioned had gotten under my skin. Or maybe it was just *him*, and his refusal to tell me anything about himself while peppering me with questions about myself. Or it was just me, and my spinning mind. Something in the story of the Monda brothers had saddened or scared me. The space between me and Angelo felt like it was filled with the invisible energy that comes from putting two magnets together the wrong way. They want to be together, yet they circle and repel each other, and you can feel the force between them and wonder which one will have to turn so they'll finally stick.

"Where are you, Danny?"

This was the type of question my mother always asked me, yet I didn't feel anger. I turned to face Angelo, whose voice was soft and gentle, and said, "I'm right here."

"No, I mean in your mind."

I couldn't figure out how to answer that, so I lied and said, "Here. I'm right here in my mind."

"You sometimes seem like you are very far away, even when you are right here."

I looked away from him toward the undersides of the umbrella pines above us and could hear the echo of my mom's answer in his words. The canopy looked like illustrations I'd seen in a science book about nerve endings in the brain. The branches were a dark cloud of nerve endings silhouetted against the silver blue of the sky. And from somewhere on the other side of the universe I could hear a voice, and it was Angelo's.

"He had been a scared young man, you know, with a wandering mind, like you." He turned to rest his head against his upper arm.

Was he talking about one of the Monda brothers, or the boy in the newspaper shop? Angelo must have realized he needed to clarify, so he said, "Dante Ferrata, the sculptor. I can tell you more about him."

"Oh," I answered. "Okay."

"Perhaps it was because he only understood stone, and how to coax impossible things out of it, but he was closed off from everyone around him. He could carve marble so it looked like human fingers digging into someone's living flesh. He could make the stone into something as intangible as a radiating halo of sunlight, and he was able to capture the breeze blowing through the leaves of a tree with his hammer and chisel. I think he loved stone so much because when he was carving, his mind stopped spinning. Everything vanished but the stone.

"Bernini took advantage of this. He practically kidnapped the boy as soon as he understood the child's genius, paying Dante's mother handsomely to let the child go. After that, Dante never stopped working. The boy didn't seem to care about anything or anyone. All he wanted to do was carve. Nothing seemed like it would ever change for him, until the day he met the little elephant. You remember the little elephant in the river?"

"Of course," I answered.

"Well, by the time Dante arrived in Tunisia in 1665, she was all grown up and had long ago been captured by humans. She'd been put to work moving huge logs all day. Dante had been sent there by Bernini to research the creatures because no elephants could be found in Italy, so he sailed to Africa, where he kept his eye out for the most beautiful example of the animal he was meant to carve. He crossed paths with our elephant on a large street in the city of Carthage at the hottest hour of the day. One look into the sad, soulful eyes of this particular elephant made something happen in Dante's heart. Something changed."

Angelo moved in the grass so his mouth was closer to my ear, whispering as if it was an important secret no one else should hear.

"Dante experienced a sensation he'd never felt before. Do you know what that sensation was?"

"No," I said.

"Neither did he . . . though I think it was . . ."

"Yes?"

"*Love.* This new feeling exposed all the emotions Dante didn't know he'd been hiding from, all the deep sorrow he'd never allowed himself to feel. He realized for the first time that he missed his mother, that he wished there were people besides the cold and ruthless Bernini to spend his days with. The time and energy he'd poured into his sculptures suddenly felt empty. The elephant taught him all of this in a fraction of a second. He felt like his knees were going to buckle.

"Dante had saved money from his work with Bernini and he managed to convince the elephant's owner to sell her. His love for her was the most real thing he'd ever felt, more real than all those blocks of marble he'd transformed, but he was still an inexperienced man. He wanted to rescue the elephant from her labors, and he believed she would want to be by his side in the distant city of Rome. He decided to leave Bernini, even though that seemed impossible, and surround himself with this new feeling he didn't have a word for."

"Love," I said, and the word echoed throughout the vaulting green cathedral of trees.

The word held us in its gravity, and we became planets circling the same sun. Just when the light seemed to be burning the brightest, Angelo's voice came to me across the farthest reaches of outer space.

"Come," he said. "It's time to visit the Mondas."

From afar, it looked like a small obelisk, but up close you could see the grave was made from marble that had been carved to look like a tall stack of books. Angelo told me it stood directly between the ancient Roman pyramid of Cestius on one side of the Non-Catholic Cemetery in Testaccio and the much smaller grave of the poet John Keats on the other side.

It had taken us a while to walk there, and I remember Angelo pointing out an American boarding school called St. Stephens on our way. For a moment I imagined what it would be like to live here, meeting Angelo when classes got out, somewhere in the endless city.

"What are you thinking about?" asked Angelo. "You are smiling."

I shrugged, and we entered the cemetery just as the golden hour was descending on the city. When the light around us hit the white marble of the book obelisk, it turned the stone a soft, glowing pink. Carved names and dates became visible on the spines of four of the marble books midway down the stack.

> *Vittorio Monda*
> *1899–1946*
> *Alberto Monda*
> *1899–*

"Danny, I'd like you to meet Vittorio and Alberto," said Angelo.

"Hello," I said to the marble.

"It's exactly five feet nine inches tall."

"What is?"

"The obelisk."

"Why?"

"Because that's how tall Vittorio Monda stood. Though not Alberto."

"But . . . weren't they identical twins? Wouldn't they have been the same height?"

"Vittorio was an inch shorter than Alberto. It happens."

"Ah," I said.

"Do you know the poems of John Keats?"

I shook my head.

The gold and pink lights were deepening. My mother expected me home soon, and it was a forty-minute walk back to the museum. Still, I didn't want to move.

"Angelo," I said, "why isn't there a death date for Alberto? Didn't he die? I thought he died."

"He had his own name and birth year carved when Vittorio died, and figured they'd just add the year of his death when he was buried, but at the end of his life he decided to be buried elsewhere."

"What happened?"

"No one knows."

"So where is he buried?"

"It's a mystery."

"They seem to be full of mysteries."

"I guess."

"Angelo," I said.

"Danny," he whispered.

"Who are you?"

Angelo smiled at my question but didn't answer. Instead, he took my hand and walked me over to a far corner of the cemetery where John Keats was buried. The grave had no name on it, just a carving of a harp with missing strings above the words, *Here lies one whose name was writ in water.* I pictured the Tiber River, and a long, dripping finger reaching up from beneath the surface to trace a vanishing name in droplets on the ground.

"Why doesn't it say 'John Keats'?" I asked Angelo, finding myself unsure that he was actually buried here. There was a lot of missing information in this graveyard.

"That's what he wanted," said Angelo. "Just this line, *'Here lies one whose name was writ in water.'* He wrote that sentence himself. But do you see the joke?"

"Joke?" I asked. "What joke?"

"Well, maybe *joke* is not the right word. A name written in water disappears quickly, evaporating to nothingness. Keats thought he was going to be forgotten. Almost no one read his poems when he was alive. He wished he could have created something that would be remembered forever. He wasn't sad, though, because he'd loved a good woman who loved him back. The words he wrote to express his disappearance are carved *in stone*, and stone doesn't disappear, at least not for many centuries. His name may not be on the grave, but it doesn't matter because everyone who comes here already knows his name. His name is writ in blood on their hearts. They come because they've read the poetry of John Keats and love him. Like Alberto and Vittorio, who came to visit him, and never left."

"Oh," I said. "That's interesting."

"No," he corrected me gently. "That's *beautiful*."

Angelo leaned very close to me. His breath was hot against my ear. I could smell some distant spice, one we'd passed in the market yesterday. *"'Beauty is truth, truth beauty,'"* he whispered. *"'That is all ye know on earth, and all ye need to know.'"*

He was quoting a famous poem by Keats, but at that moment I knew nothing, least of all what it meant. When he was done reciting, he slipped off my glasses, folded them, and put them in my shirt pocket. He then placed his hands on either side of my face. He was trembling slightly, and so was I. We both leaned forward, closer to each other. Our lips touched, and I understood what I'd been running toward all this time.

We kissed, and he tasted of honey, and figs, and Rome.

Angelo was next to me and there was no real darkness, and there was no real danger, just the understanding that I had to go home.

Of course, there was no *actual* home for me to go to, but we both knew the walk to the gates of the museum would give us more time together, while counting down to the inevitable moment we'd have to part for the night. There were no more murmurations for us because our skin stayed in contact. The electric whisper of the hairs on our arms brushing against each other created so much energy I wouldn't have been surprised if people could see us glowing in the dark.

I felt Angelo's blood racing through his veins as if it were racing through *my* veins, and I could feel his breathing as if it were in my own lungs. The moon led the way and the river rushed by somewhere in the distance. Insects called and cars whooshed down streets we couldn't see. As usual, the city was filled with people crossing bridges, holding hands, laughing, talking, playing guitars for coins in pools of light, but I didn't really notice any of them. We seemed to float from fountain to fountain, from streetlight to streetlight. The only music was the little rattle of Angelo's breath and the echo of our footsteps in the night. Closer we came to the gates, and closer, and closer.

I tried to imagine the moment of parting. There was a night guard who would be waiting, watching. He would let me in. My mother would be waiting too, wondering where I'd been, angering me with her desire to ask me questions I wouldn't know how to answer. Angelo would vanish around the corner, to some unknown region in the night. I wondered what was happening in his head. It was easy to imagine we thought the same things sometimes, but how could I know? Even if I asked him directly, there was no guarantee he'd tell me the truth, especially because I was pretty sure I would never actually say out loud most of the things I'd been thinking, not even to him. Maybe that's why silence can be so peaceful with the right person. Because it doesn't matter what you say, or what you might ask. The only thing that matters is being two bodies, together.

Before we turned onto the street where the museum waited, there was a huge stone wall, overhung with star-shaped jasmine that smelled so sweet it was hard to concentrate. Angelo, like a dancer, moved his body to face mine, and my back pressed against the wall as he pressed against me. We kissed again, this time with my glasses on, and the jasmine was in the air and his heavy breath was in my mouth, and I was so dizzy I could have fallen, but there was nowhere for me to fall.

GONE

I waited for him all the next morning, my skin growing cold as the trickle of Italians who were up early heading out for bread or coffee gave way to the usual flood of tourists and the shadow of the obelisk moved across the plaza like a huge sundial. Every time I got up to leave, I found myself sitting down again, afraid he'd arrive after I'd gone and think I'd abandoned him.

My mind raced, and the more time that passed, the more a kind of horror filled my veins. What had I done to make him stay away after the feverish few days we'd had? It felt like the ground was opening beneath me, and since I knew nothing about his real life, it made his absence feel larger and more permanent. I had no way to contact him, no way to track him down. What had I done? Was it the second kiss? Had it driven him away? I'd never kissed anyone before, so I didn't know what was supposed to happen afterward. Had it angered him somehow? That made no sense, because he'd been the one who took my face in his hands to kiss me the first time, and he'd pushed me against the stone wall to kiss me the second time too.

Oh god, I thought, *what have I done wrong?*

THE EMPTY CITY

When he didn't show up the next day either, I really began to panic.

I walked the city by myself, hoping I might run into him. I over-heard Americans talking about pickpockets and death, and there were reports about diseases and dying people that buzzed at the edges of my awareness. Though I could barely read Italian, I was sure the headlines on the papers in the newstands were all about vio-lence, and gay men and drug users dying from AIDS.

I found myself retracing the routes I'd walked with Angelo, cir-cling back again and again to the elephant obelisk, just in case he'd returned. There was an old art supply shop in Trastevere, and that afternoon I went in and bought myself a little pad and some pens. Every now and then I liked to sketch because it calmed my mind, so I started to do drawings of the Largo di Torre Argentina, the Mouth of Truth, the Colosseum, the Pantheon (whose oculus looked empty now, not full of clouds and sky as it normally did), and the giant statues at the Piazza Navona. I wandered past the towering straw-berries in the Campo de' Fiori and the mountains of spices that smelled like Angelo. I drew outside the little church by the Trevi Fountain, and I went inside, where I felt safe, lying on my back, drawing the angels. I imagined them peeling themselves from the walls after all these centuries and finding each other's warm hands in the empty air, but I couldn't bring myself to draw that. It hurt too much.

THE DREAM

Another day had passed, and then, with mounting dread, another. I dreamed the city became a landscape of ghosts, and in the dream I woke up across the ocean, in another time, and Angelo was nothing but a name in an old book my mother was trying to decipher.

THE BOOK, THE PEN, THE STAMP

I'd been a week without Angelo. My mother came back up to the apartment after her day in the lab and found me, again, lying on my couch, staring at the shadows on the ceiling.

"I'm not asleep," I said, slipping my headphones off as she tried to quietly move around the kitchen.

"Did you go out after lunch like I told you to?" she asked. She'd come upstairs during her break earlier that day and had been upset to find me still on the couch.

"No, sorry."

"Did you eat anything?"

"Not really."

I sat up and put on my glasses.

"You can't spend whole days on the couch," she said, and my only answer was a shrug. She sat next to me and put her hand on my shoulder. I wanted to push it off, to get up and run, but other than tensing my entire body, which I was sure she could feel, I didn't move. We sat there like that for what felt like a very long time, though it may have only been a few moments.

"I miss you," she said.

"I'm right here," I answered.

"You know what I mean," she said. "You can talk to me about anything, you know."

I couldn't bear her closeness. I made a shield around myself and imagined she had nothing to do with me. We were just two people who lived together. Of course, I was dependent on her in so many ways, and it wasn't until years later that I realized she might have had her own feelings of sadness and loneliness as we moved from place to place. But at the time it never would have crossed my mind that her feelings might have had something to do with *me*. I refused to imagine I might have been making her sad.

I couldn't look her directly in the eyes. I was afraid she'd be able to see Angelo somehow. Could she sense his presence in me? Could she tell what I'd done?

"What's going on?" she asked. "Are you homesick?"

"How could I be homesick?" I said. "We don't have a home."

"Hmm" was the entirety of her response, and I knew what I'd said wasn't nice. Maybe if I wasn't nice, she'd stop asking me questions. But I felt bad, so I decided to ask her a question instead. I knew she liked when I asked her something about herself, about how she'd spent her day, but the best I could come up with was the only question I ever really asked her: "How is work going?"

"Slow," she said. "Do you want to see it?"

"See what?"

"The book."

This greatly surprised me. "Really? Isn't it very delicate?"

"It is, but I've inspected it, and written up my first report. I think it can withstand the presence of a teenage boy."

She brightened up a little as she led me through the dim halls of the museum. When we got to her office, she opened the door and held it for me.

She turned on the lights, revealing a small room, stocked floor to ceiling with books and cardboard boxes. On her desk were the various magnifying lenses she used, and her handheld ultraviolet light for finding things invisible in regular light. I saw her forensic instruments, the tools of her trade. These objects always fascinated me because many of them were real medical equipment, as if she was a doctor working on sick bodies. There were razor-sharp scalpels, silver dental tools, a pair of iris scissors once used for eye surgery, and something called a bone folder. This one wasn't from the medical field, but I especially loved touching it. They'd first been made from ivory and were used to make a clean crease in folded paper, but my mom's had been given to her by a favorite teacher in grad school, Professor Banks, and was probably made from whale or deer bone.

A large window on one wall overlooked the back of the museum, though it was night now and the glass mostly served as a mirror. Our reflections looked like ghosts hovering somewhere outside in the dark garden.

"I told you about the secret panel someone found last year, and the small collection of objects that were discovered inside, along with the book."

"Yeah," I said, and my mother opened a drawer in a wood cabinet near her desk. She pulled out an amber-colored fountain pen, an ink-covered rubber stamp like you'd find in a library, and a blue cloth-covered box. She laid everything carefully on a clean white fabric on her desk.

"The treasure trove," she said. "It's okay. You can touch."

I felt nervous. I didn't want to break anything. First I picked up the stamp, which had a wood handle and a series of backward letters carved from rubber on the bottom.

"What does this say?"

My mom opened an ink pad and let me put the stamp onto the ink, then press it onto a piece of paper. When I lifted the stamp away from the paper, it said the words *Libreria de Furia*.

"What's that mean?"

"The de Furia Bookshop, essentially."

"Where is that?"

"No one knows; we can't seem to find any information. The stamp seems to be from the early 1900s, I'd guess."

I next lifted the amber pen, whose shell was translucent, and it glowed with light coming from the lamp behind it. I unscrewed the cap and looked at the nib, which had a fine line splitting the end, and remnants of dried ink.

"Does it work?" I asked.

"We haven't put ink in it, but it's in good condition. Open the box."

I put down the pen and raised the lid of the cloth-covered box. Inside was a rectangular object wrapped in clean paper. My mother put on thin white gloves from another box on her desk, as did I, and she unwrapped the paper, revealing the reason we were here. The book looked small and fragile as she placed it on her desk, yet it was powerful enough to lead us across the ocean to Rome. Without this book, there would be no Angelo, and no Danny.

The book had a faded yellowing cover, mottled with light and dark patches that might have been caused by any number of things, or so my mother had taught me over the years. Sunlight, acids, insects, water, air, heat, oil from fingertips . . . there were endless dangers if you were a book. It looked like the spine had fallen away at some point, revealing rows of carefully woven threads that bound the folded pages together. Mom allowed me to hold the book, and I had the sense I really was cradling a living thing in my hands, her newest patient. I opened the cover and held the book up to my face. I inhaled and smelled the fragrance, which was always my favorite thing to do with old books. I knew from some of my mother's other projects that mold and mildew from damp storage spaces caused the funky, musty odor of most old books. Maybe I was imagining it, but this one seemed to have a particularly sweet smell, which might have been from the wood of the secret cabinet where it was hidden for the last hundred years or so, and it reminded me of the jasmine that had scattered like stars around me and Angelo. Thinking of him, I began to tremble a little. I'm pretty sure my mother didn't notice, because she quietly told me to turn the pages, which I did.

The writing, in dark brown ink, looked as incomprehensible as my feelings.

"Do you know what it says yet?" I asked.

She laughed. "No, this is a tough one." She opened her red notebook. "I'm just starting to look at the common patterns and jot down the letter shapes that repeat in the codex." I knew *codex* was a fancy word for anything old with pages that opened like a book. My mom used the word all the time. "And because of the way the lines run," she continued with that intense look she got when her mind was working out intricate problems, "I think the original assessment that it may be poetry is probably correct." As she spoke, I noticed there were some small areas where it seemed as if someone had held a match to the surface. The inside of a few letters had also been scorched, leaving tiny letter-shaped holes through the paper.

"What happened?" I asked. "The paper looks burned."

"Good observation," said my mom. "That's exactly what happened. It's written in iron gall ink, which is a beautiful rich brown, but over time the chemicals in the ink can burn through paper. Sometimes an entire letter will separate from the page. When the book was first opened after it was found in the wall, these fell out." From a little envelope made from something I'd learned was called *glassine*, she spilled onto the desk nineteen tiny black letters, like ancient paper alphabet soup. She gave me one of her magnifying glasses, and looking at the impossibly small, scattered letters that had escaped from the book, I had the odd feeling this disintegrating object contained all my mixed-up secrets, and if my mom fully translated the text, I'd be exposed, and my life would no longer be my own. I was aware none of this actually made sense, but I had the desire to kidnap the book, destroy it, and save myself the terror of discovery. If the book no longer existed, then maybe I'd be able to carry on without anyone ever finding out about my unexplainable few days with the lost curly-haired Italian boy.

I could feel my mother watching me as I held the book, carefully turning from page to page, and I prayed she'd say nothing. I didn't want to answer any questions. I didn't want to have to put into words what I was thinking or feeling.

I just wanted Angelo.

ROOM 338

On the tenth day without Angelo, my mother made me promise again I wouldn't stay inside on the couch, so I pulled myself up after she went downstairs to work. I made my way to the gates of the museum, unsure where I was going to wander. Silvio the security guard waved me over and handed me a piece of paper folded in a triangle, saying an old woman dressed in red had dropped it off for me a little earlier.

An explosive, joyous relief rushed through me because I knew immediately who it must be from.

I unfolded the paper and discovered another hand-drawn map.

I ran as fast as I could, following the new set of landmarks Angelo had put down for me.

The grief of the past few days dissolved in the sunlight, and all that mattered was the map. It took me from the Monda Museum down through the streets of Trastevere, across another bridge, the Ponte Cestio, to a very old building on the little island in the middle of the Tiber River. It wasn't until I was inside the main entrance, surrounded by beeping sounds and hushed voices muttering in Italian and squeaking wheels rolling on dirty linoleum tiles and people dressed in loose white coats, that I realized I was in a hospital. Why would he lead me to a hospital?

All the joy that had been rushing through my body now seemed like a horrible illusion, a joke. Dread filled my chest and my throat.

My mouth dried out and my fingertips started to tingle. I checked the trembling map again, to see if I'd made a wrong turn, but I'd followed it correctly. I wasn't at the end of the route, though. I had to continue to the X, which was marked *Room 338*.

It took me a while, but I found an elevator and had to stand tight against a scuffed wall to make room for a doctor who was wheeling a patient on a large metal bed. An IV bag hung above a sick woman with yellow skin whose eyes were closed against the light. There was a smell I did not like, and I wasn't sure where to look. The elevator was slow and shaky. The lights flickered like a haunted house, and there were cigarette butts and ashes at my feet. Finally, we stopped at the third floor and the doors wheezed open. I stepped into a terribly long hallway lit too brightly with fluorescent bulbs that hung in two long rows from a dark blue ceiling. Graffiti was scratched into the plaster of the walls and there were more smells, none of them pleasant, along with a wave of dizzyingly strong bleach.

Walking slowly, not sure what I'd find when I reached the end of the map, I found myself peering into the half-open doors of the rooms I passed, giving me glimpses of scenes that looked like paintings in churches. I saw mothers weeping over loved ones, families standing in silence, old people looking out windows, and children too small to understand what was going on around them playing with dolls and toys.

I continued past all of them.

Room 335.

Room 336.

Room 337.

And then, finally, Room 338, the second-to-last room on the right.

The door was closed.

My hand hovered midair in front of the door. I couldn't move. I was afraid of what I might find inside. I was dizzy with all the sudden shifting emotions since I'd last seen Angelo, and especially the last few hours. I wasn't sure I could take many more upheavals, but I finally caught my breath and forced myself to knock. After hearing a voice answer, I turned the silver knob and stepped inside.

Directly in front of me, an old woman in a red dress was sitting beside a bed covered by a clear plastic tent attached to a large machine that pumped in pure oxygen. The machine hummed, and there was some condensation on the plastic, but I could see someone through it.

Angelo.

Something burst inside me and I wept.

The old woman turned and offered me a tissue from her purse. I could see a set of prayer beads in one hand and a plastic radio playing something tinny and operatic in the other.

"I'm . . . a friend," I said to her as I wiped my eyes beneath my glasses with the tissue she'd given me. Then I held up the map, to make it clear I was the person she'd delivered it to. I wasn't entirely sure I understood me, but Angelo said something to her in Italian. She nodded, and without a word she got up with her radio and her beads and moved to a chair in the corner of the room.

"My grandmother," he said. "She doesn't speak any English."

There were so many tubes and wires connecting Angelo's tent to the wall, and small green and red lights flashed and blinked on various monitors. But the only thing I could really see was Angelo.

He seemed pale and his hair hung limply around his face, and yet . . . and yet . . . he remained the most extraordinary person I'd ever seen. His grandmother had left a red silk scarf on the bed. Unconsciously, I began to rub my fingers against the smooth fabric. It reminded me of Angelo's skin.

"I got the map," I said. It was obvious, but I couldn't think of anything else to say at that moment.

Angelo's eyes brightened and he nodded toward his grandmother. "I convinced her to sneak a pen and paper under my oxygen tent so I could draw it for you," he said. "I swore her to secrecy, but I think she enjoyed being a spy for the morning."

I wondered where his mother was, but I didn't ask because at that moment a nurse came in to check on him. I put down the scarf and stepped back. She asked questions in Italian that he answered with short answers, then without her asking, he leaned forward so he was close to the thin wall of the tent, and the nurse checked his lungs with a stethoscope pressed against his chest through the thin, clear plastic. It was obvious they'd done this many times before. She then adjusted an IV tube, tapped her finger against a small machine, and wrote something on a clipboard. When she was done, she moved to the other patient in the room. He was a very old man, sleeping on his back. His eyes and cheeks were sunken and his white hair and stubble were glowing in the sunlight that streamed in from the smudged window behind him. It made him look like a recently martyred saint. I turned my attention back to Angelo.

"Asthma," he said to me from inside the tent. "These were particularly bad attacks. I couldn't . . ."

"I'm sorry," I said. "I didn't know."

"I have an inhaler in my pocket always, but I hid it from you as we wandered around. I didn't want you to see."

"I wouldn't have cared."

"I know. But still."

We looked at each other through the plastic for a moment, then he said, "I'm sorry it took me so long to contact you. I was in and out of the hospital, the drugs they gave me were . . . It was scary this time. I'm glad you came. I was worried you were mad at me for disappearing."

"I wasn't mad," I said as I leaned a little closer to the tent, struggling to find the right words. "How could I be mad? I was only worried."

"You really weren't mad at me?"

I smiled, which I hoped would make him believe me. "No, I was just sad. And maybe a little confused for a moment. But mostly worried. I was so happy when I got the map I ran here as fast as I could. I missed you. Are you going to be okay?"

"I'm like Rome. I've been sick forever . . . but I never die."

"When can you leave?" I asked Angelo.

"Soon, I think."

"Good," I said as I started to cry again. I took off my glasses and dried my eyes with the wet tissue and the back of my hand. Then we looked at each other through the plastic wall.

"Don't do that again," I said. "Don't disappear. Please."

"I won't," he answered, so soft I almost didn't hear it.

The nurse, having finished whatever she was doing, left the room without looking at either of us, shutting the door firmly behind her.

"Do you see it?" asked Angelo.

"See what?"

"On the table by the old man's bed. Do you see what's on it? Get up and look."

"No."

"It's okay. He's asleep."

"It's rude."

"Just do it quickly. Please."

So I stood up and looked. On the table on the other side of his bed, next to a plastic pitcher of water and a paper cup, was a small white hand, about half the size of an actual hand, its palm facing upward. I couldn't tell what it was made from. Plaster maybe, or stone, or painted wood.

I sat back down, and Angelo asked, "Does it look familiar to you?"

"The hand? No."

"It got me thinking. The photo in the brochure, of the Monda brothers. Remember it looked like they were holding something small and white?"

"Yeah."

The machinery in the room buzzed and hummed. In the corner of the room, Angelo's grandmother had closed her eyes. The music on her radio crackled, and I was glad she was asleep.

"How old do you think he is?" Angelo whispered.

"The old man? I don't know. He looked pretty old. Maybe in his seventies or eighties?" It felt strange to be talking about someone who was right next to us.

"Or almost ninety."

"I guess."

"Maybe born in 1899?"

"Maybe. Why?"

Angelo propped himself up higher and leaned closer to the plastic. "Danny, don't you understand?"

"No."

"Born in 1899. Died, unknown."

"What are you talking about?"

"The grave, Danny. This man . . ."

"Yes?"

"What if it's *him*?"

"*Who?*"

"Alberto Monda!"

I laughed. "That's not . . . Alberto died and was buried somewhere unknown. *You're* the one who told me that."

"No! It was a mystery, and what if we've solved it? What if the reason his death date isn't carved on the grave is because he's not dead?"

"The nurses have his chart. I'll ask them what his name is."

"No. Don't."

"Why?"

"Well . . . it wouldn't matter, would it? He could be using a different name now, like a spy or someone with amnesia."

And that's when I realized I could ask them about Angelo as well. With just a few questions at the nurses' station, I could probably find out his real name, and his address, and age.

I glanced toward the door, then quickly back to Angelo, who must have figured out what I was thinking. He didn't say anything, but I felt like I understood the expression that had appeared on his face. It was like I finally knew what he wanted from me, what perhaps he'd dreamed of since we first met. It was simply this: for me to agree to step into his stories, to travel with him through time and space. He wanted me to *believe* him.

Still without uttering a word, Angelo placed his open hand against the inside of the plastic, and it felt like an invitation. I mirrored him from the outside, and we pressed our palms together. We stayed like that for a long time, and I knew I wanted to be with him no matter what. I would travel with him across Rome, I'd hear his stories, I'd kiss him again, I'd believe him.

Visiting hours were almost over, and Angelo's grandmother had left a few minutes earlier. He'd drawn me close to the tent, and as he spoke, his breath fogged the plastic.

"The sea was violent and dark," he began. "Dante had arranged passage for himself and the elephant, imagining a long voyage with calm waters, but the rocking ship caused the chains that bound her to pull and cut her legs. Dante wept as he watched the torture his friend endured, and prayed it would all be over soon. He had to believe the elephant would forgive him once they'd arrived in Italy.

"When the ship finally docked in Sicily, his beloved elephant had gone nearly out of her mind. Dante did everything he could to calm her, but as she was being unloaded from the ship something went wrong with the old wooden winch that lifted her, and the rusted chains snapped.

"Unable to control herself, the elephant rampaged. Dante was seriously injured as he tried to keep the captain from pulling out his rifle. But the captain was afraid for everyone's safety, so he pushed Dante aside and, with a single shot, killed the elephant."

"Oh my god," I said.

"The tragedy destroyed Dante. Both his arms had been broken, along with his spirit. At night the elephant came to him in his dreams. It was in these dreams that he first saw the storm and the river and the elephant's rescue by her mother. He learned of the long journey up the shore after the storm ended, and he saw the body of the elephant's mother, washed up miles away. He watched as the elephant finally found her, blew dust, and covered her in leaves. Dream by dream, the life of the elephant was revealed to him.

"Months passed. Dante's arms healed before his mind. His mother, who had barely seen her son since he'd left for Bernini's, nursed him day and night, feeding him, reading to him, and bathing him. She watched as his eyes grew wide looking out the window, never knowing he was seeing the ghost of the elephant hovering in the plaza outside his window.

"Dante's mother consulted doctors and healers, and fed him a steady diet of medicines and dark roots. She fended off weekly messages from Bernini, who was less concerned about his assistant's health than he was about his own career, which had slowed considerably when he was forced to do his own work.

"Dante's suffering went on for almost a year, culminating in a terrible fever. His mother knew that at last her son was going to die. In a way she was relieved after watching him endure so much pain. Over the course of the longest night of her life, she wept and moaned beside his writhing body as she prepared herself to say goodbye.

"But in the morning a kind of miracle occurred. His fever broke, and for the first time since the accident, he spoke. He rejected his vow to leave Bernini and surround himself with love. He'd made a terrible mistake. Feeling love had brought nothing but pain and death.

He decided to leave his mother again and return to the one thing he understood. He had to carve. In Bernini's studio, the block of marble for the elephant had been waiting, and without making a single drawing or saying anything to his astounded master, he picked up his chisel and mallet, and started carving.

"Of course, no one had ever blown dust onto his beloved elephant after she died, or covered her with leaves. Without that, her ghost was trapped in the streets of Rome, forever calling to Dante in a language he would never be able to understand."

THE SCAR

The grass behind Keats's grave was cool and comfortable. Angelo's head was resting on my lap. A small candle we'd brought was burning beside us, and the marble tower of books was glowing across the way in the moonlight.

A long week had passed since Angelo had been released from the hospital and he was finally allowed back out into the city. I'd asked if I could come visit him at home—wherever that might be. But Angelo brought me here instead, so I didn't ask again.

I was very aware of the sound of his breathing now. Before he'd had his bad asthma attacks, I hadn't thought much of the fact that he'd struggled to breathe as we ran across Rome. Now, though, as we lay on the grass, I couldn't stop looking at his chest rising and falling, grateful for whatever medicines they'd given him. He was much better, but something about him seemed more delicate now. Maybe it was simply that he seemed more real. Like he was coming into focus.

I ran my fingers through his curly hair as the sounds of the city at night whispered all around us. The air felt alive and vibrant.

"Angelo?"

I knew he was listening, though he said nothing.

"How did you know I liked obelisks before we even met?"

Something shifted in his body. He glanced up at me briefly and then looked away before finally speaking.

"I saw you."

"When?"

"The day you moved in."

"But . . . how?"

He inhaled. "I live across the street from you, Danny. Across from the Monda. I saw you when you arrived with your mother. Not many young people live around there. It's mostly embassies and religious institutes on the street."

"Why didn't you just come say hello?"

"Perhaps I am shy. So I followed you, like a game."

"You're shy?" I asked, surprised. "You don't seem very shy to me."

"I am not shy with you now. But at first . . . I thought I would never talk to you. I thought I wouldn't dare. But then I saw you looking at the obelisks, and going into the church by the Trevi Fountain, and I grew unbearably intrigued. I became bolder. I made a decision. I would reach out. But still I was scared! So I led you to the map. I like maps, so I drew one for you. It was a test, to see if you would understand. And when you almost missed it, the statue said 'Wait!' and you heard it. You found the map."

I smiled. "The statue spoke? It wasn't you?"

"Maybe it was me. Maybe it was not me. But either way, Pasquino is actually known as a 'speaking statue,' though he doesn't usually speak out loud."

"Pasquino?"

"That is the statue's name. People have left notes and poems on him for hundreds of years, since he was first discovered. That's why I put the map there."

"That statue is very ugly."

"No, he is very *broken*, that is all, and don't be so quick to judge.

He brought you to me, and besides, he's not actually a sculpture of someone named Pasquino. That is just a funny name given to him many centuries ago, before archaeologists figured out what he was before he'd broken."

"What was he?"

"He was once an ancient Greek sculpture of *two* people, not one. The first man is lifting the body of a second man in battle. Look at him again the next time you walk by and you'll see the remnants of the second figure, the extra hand, the bent torso. What looks like the first man's leg is the second man's body. Pasquino is actually the memory of two men."

I moved my hand down from Angelo's hair, across his warm cheek. "How is your breathing?" I asked.

He inhaled deeply. "It is better. The thing about not being able to breathe sometimes is it makes you very appreciative of when you *can* breathe. Most people never think about breathing, but it's a miracle. A miracle that is repeated twenty-two thousand times a day, every day of your life, from birth to death. Maybe that's why people never think about it. Miracles are not supposed to happen that often."

My fingers circled his lips and then continued down across his smooth chin and his long neck, toward his chest. He stopped me, though more gently this time.

"You know you must never touch me there," he said quietly.

"Why?"

Angelo sat up and faced me. "Because . . . when I was ten, I had an operation."

"An operation? For what?"

"To fix something wrong with my . . ." He pointed to the center of his chest.

"Your sternum?"

"My sternum. I was born with an indentation in the middle of my chest, like a pit, or a deep well. I could lie on my back in the rain and fill it with water. It pressed on my heart when I had asthma attacks, and the pain . . ." He shook his head. "It was very bad. The doctors opened me up. They broke my sternum and all my ribs to lift up and remove the indentation. They sewed me up, and I spent the first three months after the operation bound tightly and stuck inside, where all I could do was read and watch movies. But then, over time, my chest became . . ."

He made a motion with his hand and I said, "Concave."

"Concave. It . . . settled inward after the operation. I became a kind of ruin."

"It hurts?"

"No, the terrible pain stopped. But now, it's hard to describe the feeling. It doesn't hurt exactly. It's more like everything is still open, like even though the doctors sewed me up and my bones have set, it feels like in my chest there is no boundary, like your hand would go through me . . . like I am the Mouth of Truth."

There was no silence in the graveyard, of course, because the sound of the wind and the distant cars never stopped, but we didn't speak for a few minutes. All I could see in my mind was my own hand disappearing into the wide-open mouth of the large stone face Angelo had taken me to visit. I could almost feel the shift in temperature as I thought about Angelo's operation. I tried very hard to imagine what he was describing, what his chest felt like to him, that sense of something not being *closed*. Once when I was little, I'd broken a finger when a friend of mine threw me a baseball I didn't catch correctly. The pain was excruciating, and it lasted a long time, though it dulled as the weeks passed. But once it was healed, it felt like it had before the break. In fact, I had forgotten about the break until now. I wondered what it would be like if some feeling never totally went away, and I was aware of it all the time. What if I never let anyone touch my hand where the break had occurred because I was afraid of the feelings?

"Angelo?" I heard my voice before I realized I'd spoken out loud. A thought had come to me.

"Danny."

"Take off your shirt."

"No."

"It's okay. It'll be okay."

"I am scared."

"I know."

I smiled, then took off my glasses and slipped my own shirt over my head. The night air felt electric against my skin. Of course people had seen me without my shirt before, but only when I'd gone swimming and had been wearing a bathing suit. Somehow it felt profoundly different to take off my shirt here, outside, in a place where you're supposed to be wearing a shirt. I felt exposed in a way I'd never felt before, but I told myself it was okay, because I was doing it for Angelo.

"Your turn," I said. "If you want. Don't be afraid."

He hesitated, but he took his shirt off as well. Immediately he hunched his back and crossed his arms in front of his chest. I gently unfolded his arms, placing them at his sides. I didn't break eye contact with him, and silently let him know I wouldn't look down without his permission. He nodded and gave me that permission.

183

His chest was like a three-dimensional map of an unknown valley, with a scar that ran almost all the way across it, like a long red river.

Angelo shivered slightly. "I dream of houses," he said as we sat facing each other with so much of our skin exposed. "Always different houses. Sometimes an apartment in Trastevere, sometimes a farmhouse, sometimes in a glass skyscraper. It is always my home, but in each dream, in each house, a wall is missing, or a window won't close, or there is an ancient road running through the living room. The house remains open, no matter what. That is what my body is like. I have no boundary, Danny. That is why I must be very cautious. I'm like Largo di Torre Argentina. If I am not careful, I might end up filled with cats."

I could tell how much effort it took for Angelo to sit like this in the candlelight, shirtless and unmoving like the angels on the ceiling of my little church. His eyes locked onto mine. I raised my right hand. I let it hover in front of his chest. He didn't move, but I could feel something change. It was like the world stopped, and the god of beginnings, transitions, and doorways appeared before us, waiting to see where we were going to go.

Angelo nodded again, and as softly as I could manage, I touched the top of his chest between his clavicles. The point of contact was small, but the world trembled. I then slowly and deliberately traced downward, into the wild valley of his body.

He gasped, and wept, and let me in.

"I mentioned a young sailor who fell into the water when the elephant rampaged," said Angelo. "Didn't I?"

I leaned against him, and he put an arm around me. As he spoke, his fingers ran gently across my chest.

"I don't remember," I managed to say. "I don't think so." I was barely able to concentrate on anything other than our skin. So much of our bodies were in contact now, it was like we were fusing together. I was so happy, so comfortable, and I felt like the only place I belonged in the world was here, right now, with him, skin against skin, in the candlelight.

"Well, either way," Angelo said, pulling me just a little tighter, as if he was aware of my thoughts, "the sailor has an important story too. I want you to know it."

"Okay," I sighed.

"His name was Giovanni Argento."

"He was on the ship with Dante?"

"Yes. But he grew up in a landlocked city in Italy, surrounded by mountains. As a child in church, he saw a mosaic of Saint Peter in a boat on the sea, and after that, he dreamed of water almost every night. When he was twelve, he secretly left home. He ran and ran until he found the shore. The first time his bare feet touched the water, he wept.

"He knew nothing of the invisible forces that ruled the tides, and as he walked deeper and deeper, he pulled off his clothes. Soon his feet no longer touched the sandy floor of the ocean. He instinctively moved his arms and legs until he was swimming. The more he swam, the farther out he was carried by the unseen tide. The world he knew vanished along the horizon until everything around him was vast and bright and blue."

I hadn't realized it at first, but the sound of the breeze and the story Angelo was telling me had run together, and his words had given way to the images they evoked, so it seemed as if I was *myself* now adrift on the vast ocean, and I could actually hear it roaring around me, and the world was thrilling, bright daylight.

"There was a kind of peace in the water," came Angelo's voice. "Giovanni didn't understand that salt was buoyant, so his ability to float effortlessly felt magical and calming. Beyond dreaming of the water, he had never thought much about the future. His mother had told him many stories, and they usually ended with a trip to paradise or a descent into hell. Now that he'd found the ocean, he thought perhaps he'd reached his own kind of paradise, and all that was left for him was this: his body floating in the water until he died.

"Above him, clouds made wonderful shapes across the sun and birds circled like loose kites. Below him were the shadows of large fish that turned his thoughts to Jonah and the whale. He wondered if he might be swallowed whole, and live out his days in the belly of a leviathan at the bottom of the sea. His mind began to drift in much the same way as his body, and after several hours, or months, or years, he heard the voice of God.

"God had an unidentifiable accent and sounded very far away. Giovanni turned to face the Lord Almighty and found himself confronted with a towering wall that had appeared in the middle of the water like a miracle. But the wall was a ship, and the voice was a man who was being lowered in a lifeboat, and the naked, delirious child was brought in from the darkening sea."

I must have gasped because Angelo stopped and turned to me. "Are you okay?" he asked.

"Yes, sorry," I said, unsure how to tell him I'd become so much a part of the narrative that it felt like I myself was being lifted naked from the waters.

"Please," I said, turning against his body while remaining cautious of his chest. The heat between us grew. "Go on."

Angelo ran his palm up my arm. "Giovanni, perhaps a little out of his mind, told the crew he'd been born in the water and if he touched land he would die. No one was sure if they believed him, but unwilling to take chances with fate, they treated him like he'd been sent by Heaven, or like he was some kind of strange gift from the sea. He was given whatever he wanted, but as he came to his senses, the only thing he wanted was to work on the ship and earn his keep. He asked to stay aboard when they docked, and when he needed to move on to another ship, he was given a small rowboat to take him so he wouldn't have to touch the dry earth.

"Giovanni lived like this, ship to ship, wave to wave, storm to storm, for ten blissful years. But everything changed on a voyage from Africa to Italy, when a man with an elephant came on board. Giovanni, like most people outside Africa and India, had never seen an elephant before, and he'd never seen a man like Dante Ferrata, fiery eyed and intense, like the old saints from the Bible who burned with passion for God, but that passion in Dante was directed toward this great gray creature, a living monument, a walking, breathing house with a soul.

"Giovanni became obsessed with this unusual man and his even more unusual elephant. Whenever possible he'd wait outside Dante's cabin, or follow behind him when he took walks on the deck. Dante noticed the young sailor with the golden skin who always seemed to be hovering around him, and one night he invited Giovanni into his cabin. Before long, the two men became inseparable, and others on the ship treated them with reverence, as if Dante had been chosen from the flock by someone holy. At night, inside the cabin, candles cast a warm glow over everything. As the ship rocked, Giovanni would look at papers that were scattered across all the surfaces of the room, words spilling out in black ink. Dante, who had been writing passionately about the elephant each night, didn't know that Giovanni had never learned to read, so he would push the papers aside and say, 'Words are not what matters now,' and then he'd blow out the candles one by one."

I wasn't sure when Angelo's voice had stopped, exactly, but at some point, as our bodies settled further into each other, I realized the only sound I could hear was our breathing. We'd left Giovanni and Dante in their darkened room, where they could do whatever they wished to do. So, with their story burning brightly in my mind, I leaned over and blew out our single candle, leaving the two of us alone in the open air, to do whatever we wished to do.

THE SWEET LIFE

In the silvery light of a distant night, a goddess in a black dress and a white shawl was floating through the empty streets of Rome, a small white cat perched carefully on her head. She moved through the shadows of a stone passageway, the long hem of her gown sweeping behind her. Emerging from the mysterious archway, she gently removed the cat, and the shawl, and walked directly into the moonlit waters of the Trevi Fountain, as if she'd come home. No one was allowed to enter the fountains of Rome, but it was the middle of the night and no one was around. No one, that is, except for a man with tousled hair who had always loved her. He removed his shoes, but not his dark suit, and entered the fountain to be near her, to touch her. She dipped her hand into the pool and baptized him with a few drops, as the water falling from the stone giants above them cascaded and roared all around.

I turned to Angelo, whose eyes were glistening in the reflected light from the movie screen, and he pressed his knee against mine. Our hands, hidden by the darkness, gripped each other tightly. "Come," he'd said earlier. "There's a place I like to go when the heat becomes too much," and he'd brought me here, to this small, dusty movie theater on a side street deep in the middle of Trastevere. Fading posters and photographs from old Italian movies covered its walls. The carpet was blue and threadbare down the center from decades of footsteps. There was the burnt smell of popcorn in the air, and the woman behind the cracked glass and bronze ticket booth had looked as if she'd been there since the theater opened in 1921. The movie we were watching was one Angelo had seen a few times on VHS and television, but never in a theater.

"It's called *La Dolce Vita*," he'd said to me. "Do you know what that means?"

I shook my head.

"*The Sweet Life*," he'd answered, with a smile that said it was the perfect title, and the perfect movie for us to see together in an air-conditioned theater in the middle of the hot summer.

There were a few very old people in the audience, but mostly the place was empty. We sat in the back, in a row by ourselves, where the velvet seats were soft against the skin of our legs, and the floor was sticky and hard. The air was as cool as Angelo had promised, and it was a relief to find myself chilly. We pushed our arms against each other, and the heat from his skin felt extra nice.

The movie was long, and black-and-white, and I didn't understand anything they said. Angelo tried to translate for me by whispering close to my ear, but his hot breath was distracting and I began to feel like I had fallen into a dream. On screen, there was the blond goddess in the fountain, and long, swirling, wild parties. There were visits to the Vatican, and the ruins of ancient baths, and secret clubs, and old men and young women and drives in cars, and a castle, and the deaths of two children, and shirtless young fishermen on a beach at dawn who catch a sea monster in their endless nets. And through it all was the man with the tousled hair who'd been baptized by the goddess in the fountain. On the beach, after inspecting the sea monster, he waved goodbye to a girl he didn't really know and walked off with his friends. The girl on the beach was left alone, watching him as the wind blew her hair, and Angelo and I watched her as she watched him, and the lights came up, and our bodies parted, and the world outside was waiting.

OSTIA

After a few more blissful days with Angelo, I awoke to find my mother up earlier than usual and already sitting at the kitchen table. Large unfolded maps and open guidebooks were spread out in front of her. "Morning," she said as I rubbed my eyes and found my glasses.

"What are you doing?" I asked.

"I have a little surprise."

"A surprise? For what?"

"Remember you said you wanted to go beneath the Colosseum, into the labyrinth where the warriors and the animals waited before the fights?"

"I did?"

"Yes, you did. When we were packing, and I was telling you about Rome."

"Oh. Okay."

"Well, you wanted to see it, even though it's not open to the public. A few weeks ago I met an archaeologist who was visiting the museum, and she's doing work there and has a set of keys. Imagine having keys to the Colosseum. I didn't tell you until she'd confirmed because I didn't want to disappoint you, and then last night she called to tell me the only time she could meet us before she leaves town is this morning. I arranged to take half the day off so we could go have a little adventure."

"But . . ."

"But *what?*"

"I can't."

I could feel the air being sucked out of the room. "What do you mean you can't?" asked my mother, with something like a laugh in her voice.

"I can't. I mean. I, uh. I have plans."

"With who?"

"With no one. It's just. There's something important I was going to do today, and I really have to do it."

She sighed and sat up a little straighter. "You're annoying me."

"I know. I'm sorry."

"Dr. Magnani is doing us a favor."

I hated when she got like this, when she expected something from me that I didn't want to give her. I hated it so much.

"I know," I answered.

"I never take time off from work."

"I know."

"I really wanted to . . ." She paused, then closed the guidebook she'd been thumbing through and looked at me from across the room. I was sitting up now at the edge of the couch, wearing an old blue tank top, with the thin sheet I slept beneath pulled over my lap. Neither of us moved. It was like waiting for a car to crash. But at the last minute my mother took control of the steering wheel. She collected everything she'd laid out on the table, got up, and said, "I'll call and tell Dr. Magnani we can't make it. Something's come up." She went into her bedroom without looking at me, and a few moments after that I heard the front door open and close. I hadn't realized I'd been holding my breath. I exhaled, and decided that none of this mattered at all. I hurried to get dressed, grabbed a quick bite to eat, and ran out the door.

I somehow got to the elephant obelisk early. I was pacing back and forth, trying not to think about the morning, when I heard the sound of a motorbike. This was not unusual; Rome was filled with motorbikes. The bigger ones, which shone in various candy colors, were called Vespas, but there were a billion smaller ones flying around the city called Ciaos. But the roar of this particular Ciao (pronounced *Chow*, the Italian word for *hello*) was particularly loud and grating, like a lawn mower, and the sound was getting closer and closer to me, until it was so close I thought if I didn't turn around I might get run over.

A baby-blue bike came to a stop just feet from where I was standing, and to my shock the driver was Angelo. He was grinning like he'd won the lottery, and he had a heavy chain with a padlock slung across his shoulder. With a tilt of his head I climbed on the seat, squeezing myself on behind him, and the morning disappeared so completely it was like I'd never had a mother at all.

"Where did you get this?" I asked, astonished, but instead of answering we just sped off as I wrapped my arms tightly around him. Being careful of his chest, I grasped his stomach and pressed my legs as hard as I could against the sides of his legs.

"Where are we going?" I yelled into his ear, but he continued to say nothing. The vibration of the bike on the cobblestones and streets made my teeth chatter and my head spin. I was sure I'd fall off at any moment, and no one wore helmets in 1986. But his long, curly hair smelled of apples and his neck tasted of salt, so for two hours I grasped his sweating body as his damp curls brushed against my face, my eyes, my skin, my lips. It felt like we were flying.

We passed a sign for a town called Ostia, turned sharply, and eventually found a place to lock up the bike. It turned out we were going to the beach.

"Maybe we'll find a sea monster, like in the movie," Angelo said.

Our bodies were still vibrating from the ride, but we took off our shoes the second we got to the sand and looked out across the flock of people who'd arrived before us. Everywhere in Rome, boys walked together with their arms around each other's shoulders, and all across the shore they seemed to travel together in shirtless, shouting murmurations. So we took their lead and kept our arms around each other the whole day. I took off my shirt, and looked at Angelo, who seemed to have suddenly remembered people removed their clothes at the beach. I nodded encouragingly and he took a deep breath. He lifted his shirt up over his head and dropped it along with mine on the towels he had packed. I took off my glasses, carefully folded them into a pocket, and then, wearing just our shorts, we ran together into the sea, where we laughed and struggled to keep hold of each other as we dove through the waves, though I remained careful of his chest the entire time. The water was blue and green and cool, and the sun shimmered across the surface as far as we could see, glittering like falling stars. Boats glided across the horizon, triangular white sails moving back and forth, and when the water was over our heads, we'd swim back and I'd nervously make sure his breathing was still okay.

We tumbled out of the water toward our towels and fell down to the ground, sparkling and exhausted. Side by side, we sighed and breathed, our arms up over our heads, our feet skimming against each other, the smell of suntan lotion wafting in from somewhere nearby. After a few moments, I realized Angelo had not put his shirt back on. He was lying on his back, leaving his chest exposed for the world to see, the drops of water on his golden skin rolling and gathering down toward the ribbon of his scar.

Soon he turned over and rested his head on his hands, his face toward me. I turned over too, and positioned myself so our elbows were in contact. His tongue flicked against the small chip in his front tooth. I gazed at the flecks of green in his eyes, the long black lashes, and the fine light hairs that grew down the center of his spine and up the back of his neck, which I discovered that moment at the beach. They all thrilled me like nothing I could ever have imagined. I closed my eyes and his name moved through my mind like a starling. Without realizing it I must have spoken his name out loud, because he said, "Danny." But when I looked toward him, I saw his eyes were shut. He'd spoken my name in his sleep.

I watched the gentle rise and fall of Angelo's back. The sound of the pounding waves roared ceaselessly behind us, and the smell of salt was everywhere, and the heat of the sun baked my skin—nearly all of which was exposed to the air. It was like I really had become Giovanni, and I'd just arrived at the moment he first walked naked into the water. It must have been a beach not unlike this one, and water not unlike the water Angelo and I had just been playing in. Giovanni had spent his life dreaming of the ocean, and when he found it, and entered it, everything suddenly made sense. He'd found the place he most belonged, even if it might lead him to his death. But it didn't lead him to his death. It led him to Dante. And somehow I was led to Angelo.

How was any of this possible?

I felt like I was living a kind of sideways life, one that had accidentally been slipped into my regular, unhappy life. In the real world there was my mother and her needs and her expectations and her endless work. I was alone there, somewhere in another room, unable to even dream of anything different. But she and I had come to Rome, and a map had appeared, which led me through a crack in the world into another universe, and even though there was a time limit to the invisible passport I'd been issued, I was happy. The one thing I was unable to imagine was bringing these two dimensions together. My future—at least once I got back to America—felt like a bleak one, where I'd be forced into a familiar loneliness that was foreign to me here, on the beach, next to Angelo.

ALBERTO MONDA

In the center of Trastevere is a plaza with an eight-sided stone fountain. There are seven steps on each side that people sit on at all times of the day and night eating pizza and gelato, sipping coffee and gossiping with their neighbors. On one side of the plaza is an old church and on the other is a five-story building with ancient shuttered balconies and a café on the ground floor. Many evenings, after we had wandered together through the city, Angelo and I would join the others on the steps of the fountain to rest. After we came back from Ostia we'd compare the color of our arms, enjoying the opportunity it gave us to touch each other in front of other people. My mom hadn't asked me anything the night I'd come back from the beach, though she must have noticed my sunburn because I found a tube of aloe on the sink the next day.

Even though she worked most of the time, she continued to circle me in the mornings and at night in a way that made me nervous. It was tiring inventing an entire fictional life for myself, but it seemed obvious to me she'd never understand what was going on. So I continued to remove Angelo from my days, telling stories about lonely rambles through the crowded city, stumbling by accident upon interesting places I then researched in guidebooks I read in bookstores. In the version of my life I created for my mother, I had taught *myself* to drink espresso, and roamed on my own through the fruit stalls of the Campo de' Fiori.

In the meantime, Angelo and I spent all our days together. We continued going to the movies, and he was teaching me some Italian so I was able to follow a little more of the stories. Even the American movies were dubbed into Italian, and Angelo tried to fill me in on what I missed, not that it really mattered. I just liked being in the cool darkness beside him, our hands together. Afterward we'd walk over to the Trastevere fountain, where we'd sit and talk. But we also grew comfortable in silence together. My skin always hummed whenever I was near him, and the tingle of our hands grazing each other as we made our way through the city, or catching his eye on a crowded corner as we found each other again, was always deeply satisfying and secretly thrilling.

Other people's conversations buzzed in the air, but we barely ever heard them. Young men in sleeveless shirts endlessly whirred around us on their Ciaos and Vespas, and dogs barked from unseen corners. We'd eat pizza and share a lemon gelato, our feet touching in such a way that it was invisible to everyone but us, and we felt secure that no matter who walked by, our secret would not be guessed, or ruined, or shattered.

One twilight, as the piazza around the fountain burst in shocking gold, I finally got him to talk a little more about his family. Earlier that day we had tried once more to visit the room at the bottom of San Clemente, but we'd found a new chain and lock on the gate. We weren't sure if it was a coincidence, or if someone had become suspicious, but suddenly we wanted to be somewhere private, and the graveyard was open to the public during the day. "What about your home?" I asked nervously. "Can we go there?" In response to this question, he laughed. "There is never any privacy," he said. "So many people live with us. Aunts, and cousins, and my grandmother of course."

"How long have you lived there?"

"The apartment has belonged to my family for many generations. And sometimes it feels like no one has ever moved out."

I was going to try to ask him about his mother again when Angelo's eyes suddenly darted to something behind me and he visibly shivered. I started to turn, to see what he was looking at, but he stopped me with his hand.

"It's him," he said.

"Who?"

"The old man from the hospital. Alberto Monda."

"That wasn't Alberto Monda."

"Well, maybe, maybe not, but he's there, by the policemen."

Angelo nodded toward them, and I thought I may have briefly seen someone with white hair, but Rome was filled with old people, and light was glinting on something shiny, like eyeglasses perhaps, so I wasn't sure who Angelo had seen.

"It's him, I'm telling you," he said, jumping up and pulling me to my feet. "Come on."

"What are you doing?"

"Let's follow him!"

"Angelo! There's no one there." But Angelo wouldn't listen. Before I could say another word, he'd darted into the crowd.

"Angelo," I called. "Don't run!"

I headed in the direction he'd gone, though I could no longer see him. Soon I got a brief glimpse of him as he turned a corner, and I ran past a little shop selling hand-painted tiles for tourists, across another piazza, and then down a small road where a man was sitting on a small bench fixing a guitar in front of a shop hung with what seemed like thousands of broken stringed instruments.

"Angelo!" I shouted down the road, worried again about his breathing. "Stop!"

At a little intersection where four cobblestone streets radiated outward like a twisted star, I looked down each road, unsure which way to go. A white truck trundled by, so close I had to push myself up against a wall, and when it passed I saw Angelo standing across from me, as if the truck had made a special delivery.

"He got away," Angelo said, out of breath.

"Do you want to have another asthma attack?" I asked. A kind of panic had overtaken me. "Take your medicine," I insisted, then caught myself and added, "Please."

Angelo looked at me with a funny squint in his eye. "I took it," he said. "I know when to take my medicine. You sound like my mother."

"I'm sorry. I'm just worried," I replied. Then I paused for a moment before adding softly, "You don't need to make up adventures for me. I'd want to be with you even if we did nothing at all."

"*Make up* adventures? What are you talking about?"

A wave of heat rolled across my body. I'd said the wrong thing and wasn't sure what to do.

"Do you think I lied to you?"

"No, Angelo. I'm sorry. I believe you. I . . ."

I wanted to say more, but everything in my mind grew confused. I didn't want to cry again, and even more I didn't want to upset him.

I also didn't want him to run, and I didn't want him to have an asthma attack again. I didn't want him to die.

I realized I had to dry my eyes. Pushing my fingers beneath my glasses, I wiped away the unwanted tears. Once my eyes had focused again, I looked at Angelo for a long moment. There was something so gentle and needful in his expression, and then all at once a magnificent idea clicked into place, so completely that it felt as if the gears of my mind had actually made a sound.

"Angelo," I said.

"Yes, Danny?"

"What are you doing at midnight tonight?"

THE SECRET ROOM

"Shh," I whispered as Angelo came through the basement window. It had taken me some time during the afternoon, but I finally figured out how I could sneak him into the Monda. Then, when my mother had fallen asleep, I tiptoed out of the apartment just before midnight, candle in hand, and went to a small window in the basement. From the inside, the window was high up the wall, but from the outside, where Angelo was waiting, just as I'd told him, it was almost level with the ground. He slid through legs first, and it was like he was materializing from another dimension.

And then I shared with him my grand idea.

I led him by the flickering light through the basement to the closed door of the storage room. I pointed to the knob, indicating he should open it, which he did.

It was like stepping into Oz, and I said, "No one will find us here."

The wild tumble of boxes and books and furniture took on a kind of life, like a forest of possibilities. The giant map presided over the whole place, and Angelo turned to me with awe in his voice. "It's really ours?"

"As far as I know, only Vee the cat knows about this place. And look," I said as I shut the door. "It locks."

We lit some candles I'd tucked into my pocket and set to work. We cleared one corner of the room, lifting and moving a heavy desk and some empty filing cabinets. We found a large bulletin board against

205

one wall. It still had a few old articles pinned to it, but we slid it out and laid it across the top of the furniture to form a sort of secret space within the secret space. If anyone did have a key and came inside unexpectedly, we'd remain hidden and safe.

"Is there anything soft around here?" he asked, and soon we'd unearthed a couple of tattered blue cushions from toppled armchairs. We placed the cushions on the floor of our little space and set up some boxes and piles of books like tables. We found a little souvenir sculpture of Romulus and Remus and the she-wolf on a marble base, which we set up near the cushions.

Angelo smiled. "Home," he said, and then to my surprise he took off his shirt. I took off mine, and my chest fit perfectly into his chest, like the last two pieces of a puzzle. Our hearts beat side by side, and my tongue found the little chip in his left front tooth.

We decided to mark the giant crumbling map with all the places we'd been together, like a diary of our summer. We circled the museum, the Pantheon, the elephant obelisk, the kingdom of cats, San Clemente, the hospital on the little island, and the fruit stalls of Campo de' Fiori. We estimated where the cafés and gelato shops were since they were the only places not on the seventeenth-century map, but the streets were pretty much all the same. We both had pens in our hands and added more and more circles, laughing and remembering each step we'd taken, the grove of umbrella pines in the park, the riverbank we'd walked, the bridges we'd crossed, but then, at the very same moment, we both froze. Our eyes locked and somehow I felt he was thinking what I was thinking . . . the more we filled in the map, the more days that passed, the fewer hours we'd have left together. August fifth was hurtling toward us, less than four weeks away, and no matter how hard we tried to run in the other direction, to avoid clocks and calendars, the summer was going to come to an end.

So what could we do with the pain growing in our bodies that threatened to overwhelm us if we thought too much about it? We did the only thing that made sense to us. We would spend our time forgetting. We had a home now, a nest that was just ours, in a sea of blue cushions. Eventually we would bring down more blankets and pillows, but no matter how terrified we were about the end of the summer, no matter how scary the world became, we now had a place where we could lie together, side by side, holding each other tightly, skin against skin, to kiss, and touch, and whisper stories in the dark.

"Giovanni started to have terrible dreams the closer the ship came to Italy. He dreamed of monsters and demons, floods and infernos, and Dante tried to calm him during the night. In the morning it was Dante who worried, afraid his elephant wouldn't be happy in her new home. The young sailor thought only of Dante, but the former sculptor's thoughts were filled with his giant beast.

"Like many tragedies, the tragedy of the elephant felt inevitable, as if fate had created Dante and Giovanni and the elephant for this one horrible moment. Giovanni was thrown overboard by the rampaging elephant, and after the captain had killed it with the blast of his gun, Dante's screams suddenly stopped. Giovanni was pulled back on board the boat, and his friend's silence terrified him more than his earlier cries. The young sailor didn't remember much after that. The man he loved was taken away, and Giovanni was brought down to the cabin they'd shared for so long. He refused to allow anyone to touch the papers left behind by his friend, who'd continued to write each night, relighting the lanterns after the two men had spent long hours in the dark. When the ship was repaired and finally ready to sail again, Giovanni gathered the papers into a pile, put them in a leather bag, and, for the first time since he was a child, set foot onto the solid earth.

"For the next several years he tried to track down Dante. The task was made nearly impossible because even though they'd spent so much time together aboard the ship, Dante had never once mentioned stone, or chisels, or carving, so Giovanni knew nothing of the central fact of his friend's previous life.

"Giovanni traveled from city to city, town to town, asking after an injured man who had loved an elephant, but all he was met with were blank and curious stares. When he came upon a small town filled with bookbinders, he had the pages he carried bound together to keep them safe. This book became a holy relic for Giovanni, and every night he'd wonder what it said. He dreamed of the moment he'd be able to deliver the book back into Dante's hands and Dante would read him the mysterious words.

"Eventually, Giovanni found himself in the vast, chaotic city of Rome. So much time had passed that he'd pretty much given up on ever actually finding his beloved. But he had vowed not to return to the sea as long as he held on to the book, and the only way to get rid of the book was to give it to Dante. He was stuck.

"One day by chance he walked past the Pantheon and came upon a long trench in the Piazza della Minerva where a broken obelisk had been unearthed. As he stared down upon it with wonder, he heard men talking nearby. They spoke of long-delayed plans for the obelisk to be resurrected and mounted on the back of a marble elephant. It was to be carved by the great sculptor Gian Lorenzo Bernini.

"In a flash Giovanni somehow knew this would lead him to his friend. It didn't take him long to track down the studio of the famous sculptor. A few questions led him back to a large room where a familiar-looking elephant with an extraordinary expression was emerging from a vast block of white marble. From behind the ghostly creature stepped Dante, a chisel in one hand, a hammer in the other.

"'Your name is Bernini now?' asked Giovanni.

"'Bernini is my master,' said Dante.

"Giovanni immediately knew something was wrong. His friend's eyes, once blazing with passion and love, now seemed empty and distant.

"'Dante,' said Giovanni as he fumbled in his bag. 'I've brought you the writing you left on the ship. I've bound the pages together in a book. Take them.'

"'No,' said Dante coldly. 'My master commands I make this statue. Once it is done I shall banish from my memory everything connected with the elephant and that terrible journey.'

"'But I was part of that journey, Dante. Do not banish me from your memory too.'

"'It is too late, Giovanni. I died on the ship with the elephant. That writing is no longer mine.'

"'You are not dead, you are standing here before me, speaking and breathing, as real and alive as the book in my hands.'

"'My soul is dead, Giovanni. I am stone.'

"Giovanni fell to his knees, tears in his eyes. 'Dante,' he said. 'Please. Many years have passed but I am the same person, and so are you.'

"'You are wrong,' said Dante Ferrata. 'Neither of us is the same person. The Giovanni Argento I knew had not walked on dry land since he was a child, and I was not a stone carver aboard that ship. You must leave here. Go back to the ocean and never return.'

"'But I've searched all of Italy for you.'

"'You were searching for a ghost,' said Dante, and with that he turned his back on Giovanni, raised his hammer, and continued to carve the marble elephant, and Giovanni disappeared into the night."

"What happened to him?" I wanted to know.

"Have you heard of the Shadow of the Boat?" asked Angelo.

I shook my head.

"Well, people began reporting that they saw a dark figure near the Fountain of the Broken Boat at the base of the Spanish Steps. We've passed it in our travels."

"I remember."

"It commemorates something that really happened once in Rome," he continued. "A ship came loose from its moors and floated through the streets of the city after a flood, and it came to rest on that very spot."

"Really?"

Angelo nodded. "Then, around the time Giovanni disappeared," he continued, "the dark figure appeared by the fountain. This figure became known as the Shadow of the Boat, and could usually be spotted after midnight walking with a book under his arm. The figure would circle the stone boat several times, then step into the water. He was said to live in a narrow building to the right of the Spanish Steps, because each night he'd leave watery footprints to the door. But within a year or two all sightings of the figure with the book stopped and he became another one of the many legends that fill the impossible purgatory of Rome. And, Danny?"

"Yes, Angelo?"

"A hundred and fifty-three years after that, John Keats died in that same building, at the base of the Spanish Steps, listening to the gurgling water of the Fountain of the Broken Boat. They say it was the sound of that very fountain that inspired him to write the words we saw on his grave: *'Here lies one whose name was writ in water.'*"

Again I pictured a finger writing a name with water from the Tiber River, but now the name was *Giovanni*, and soon the finger wrote a second name: *Dante*. I thought about how they had lost each other as I saw the names evaporate into the air and one day, before too long, I knew I was going to lose Angelo too. But at this moment, on our blue sea of cushions, I still had him, and his body was warm, and the dawn was very far away.

MUSIC

I'd bought my small black cassette player at a Radio Shack in Ohio a couple of years earlier, with birthday money I'd been saving. I'd been visiting the Radio Shack for weeks, staring at all the different display models on shelves attached to the walls, talking to the guy who worked there about this brand and that brand, dreaming about the exotic accessories you could also buy, like fancy microphones and external speakers and stereophonic headphones, though I knew everything needed to be easy to travel with as I moved from place to place with my mother.

I loved the little recorder I finally purchased; the weight of it in my hand, pushing the little copper-colored batteries into the secret compartment on the bottom, the sound the buttons made when I pressed them, the way the little door slid open like a hatch on a spaceship with a wonderful clicking sound, and how neatly the cassettes fit into the slots in the door. I loved pushing the door closed and recording music off the radio. It's hard to imagine now, but we had to wait for songs to play on the radio and then press the "record" button at just the right time in order to capture the songs we didn't already own on cassette. I usually lived in college towns with my mom, which meant there were always great student-run radio stations playing new and obscure bands. I had some tapes of classical music my mom had introduced me to, like Bach and Ravel, but my favorites were bands I'd

213

discovered through these radio stations, like the B-52's, The Cure, The Smiths, Sparks, Felt, and New Order.

Each night, I'd take the player and box of cassettes down to our secret room so I could play everything for Angelo. I spent hours choosing songs I thought he'd like, and the music became our backdrop, our landscape, our secret language. We'd quote lyrics to each other, and we'd dance together, singing and laughing, until we fell down onto our soft blue nest and we eventually wouldn't be singing or laughing anymore. But the music would continue, and the rhythms would change and the beat would grow strong and then pull back until everything was soft and entrancing, and the next song would begin and the drums and the electronic tempo would rise and rise and it would feel as if the music was being driven by the pumping of our hearts and the thoughts in our heads, until there was no difference between what we heard and what we saw and what we felt, and I'd change the tapes and no matter what I put on, every song was about us, and we'd listen as the candles would gutter and burn.

I Melt with You
    The Boy Who Came Back
        Just One Kiss
            Angels and Devils
                This Night Has Opened My Eyes
                    Thieves Like Us
                        I'll Tumble 4 Ya
                            Cool Places
                                Perfect Skin
                                    Leave Me with the Boy . . .

ELIJAH AND ISAK'S STORY

When the iron gate shut behind us, the vestibule was plunged into shadows. Dim, dusty light filtered in from somewhere above the huge wood doors, and a set of old metal mailboxes was visible to the left. Paint was peeling off the walls in wide chunks, exposing layers of other paint, wallpaper, and stone beneath it. The ceiling was high and a small glass fixture with a broken bulb hung in the center from the end of a long rusty chain. The space was deep and empty, except for a collapsing wooden chair in the distance and a pile of Italian newspapers and magazines collecting by the mailboxes.

"Angelo," I whispered. "Where are you going? Your eyes are playing tricks on you. No one came in here."

But he pointed ahead into the darkness. Three more times we'd been sitting on the fountain in the center of Trastevere when Angelo said he'd spotted the old man from the hospital. Given what had happened the first time, I followed him without complaint, but I continued to see nothing. This time, though, he said the old man had entered this old building at the corner of the square. In the darkness of the entryway, I really couldn't figure out where Angelo thought he was going, because the space seemed to have no exits except the one we'd come through. But as we walked into the dim corner, our eyes adjusted and the room opened up, revealing the bottom of a wide wooden staircase leading up into the darkness. Each step was a triangle and the stairs turned around a central axis.

"He must have gone up here," whispered Angelo.

As we climbed, we passed boarded-up windows and piles of moldering boxes left long ago in the corners. Angelo squeezed my hand tightly and pulled me upward. The first landing we came to had a huge green door with a padlock firmly affixed to the handle, and the second landing had the same door and the same padlock. Up we went, step by step, until we came to the fifth floor at the top of the building. The large green door on this landing was slightly ajar.

Angelo's breathing had become a little labored and for the first time he let me see him use the inhaler he pulled from his pocket. I knew I shouldn't say anything, so we waited for the medicine to open up his breathing. I wanted desperately to turn back, and even though I'd said nothing, Angelo could sense what I was thinking. His eyes widened into a kind of plea, and I couldn't resist him.

The door was very heavy and we pushed it open as quietly as we could until our bodies were able to fit through the space. His breathing was still a little loud, which continued to worry me. It was the only sound as we entered a small area, a little hallway that was empty except for a single framed black-and-white tourist postcard of the Pantheon. At the end of the space was another door, this one small and red. Angelo pulled my hand, and we had the following silent conversation as I pulled backward.

We really should leave. This is trespassing!

No, let's keep going. Trust me.

He kissed me briefly on the lips, and won.

We tiptoed to the door and silently turned the brass knob. He went through first, and I followed, still hand in hand, my heart beating hard.

Moonlight flooded in through open shutters, casting everything in silver and blue. The room looked like someone a hundred years ago had bought the contents of an antique shop, a museum, an office, and an artist's studio, tossed them together, and then just carried on collecting more things. The walls were lined with sagging book-shelves, while piles of other books teetered nearby. Paintings of landscapes and gods covered the rest of the walls up to the ceiling, and I noticed a large framed engraving of a young man looking dreamily upward as he leaned his chin on the palm of his hand. It was labeled: *John Keats, Poet, 1795–1821.*

"I think he's following us," I said.

"My mother studied him in college," whispered Angelo.

This was the first time he'd said something specific about her, and it felt significant, like a little clue in a vast mystery had fallen into place, and Keats had so much to do with . . . us.

There were old postcards and cutout newspaper articles taped to open areas of plaster. Throughout the room stood islands of filing cabinets of every shape and size, and wedged in a corner were piles of arms and legs from antique mannequins. Plaster models of churches and bridges gathered on tables that were also covered with jars of paint, and salvaged pieces of architecture, wooden gargoyles, and ornate silver light switches. Everywhere you looked there was another encyclopedia's worth of objects, telling all sorts of mixed-up stories. Children's clay pots were piled near antique eyeglasses; decaying silk top hats sat beneath flags of unknown nations, and tattered silk hang-ings swayed in the slight breeze that blew in from the open windows. And glowing throughout the space were white marble sculptures, some smooth, round, and abstract, while others were realistic figures that looked like mythological heroes or sleeping heroes. Multicolored Moroccan glass lamps hung from the ceiling, and chains made of fading construction paper from some long-ago party were still taped to the top edges of the bookcases.

The light subtly shifted in the room and we turned back toward the doorway. To my shock, standing there, in murky silhouette, was the old man from the hospital, just as Angelo had said. He wore gold glasses now, and had his white hair parted neatly to one side. The three of us stared at one another, as if none of us knew what to do or say. We'd been caught and there was nowhere to run. He was blocking the door. Nothing moved in the room except the tattered silks and the glittering dust caught in the otherwise invisible eddies of the air.

Without saying a word, the old man moved toward us. He had a slight limp and listed a little to the right as he walked. Angelo and I instinctively let go of each other's hands and stepped apart, and to our surprise he just shuffled between us, as if we were ghosts. Frozen now with something between terror and curiosity, we watched as he navigated the narrow paths of the furniture and objects that filled the space. He made his way to an overstuffed leather chair I hadn't noticed.

Before he sat down, he turned on a standing lamp whose bulb flickered on, giving off a faint gold light. He inhaled, removed his glasses, and rubbed his eyes. There was a book on a table next to the chair, which he picked up, opened, and began to read. I took a step back, eager to go, and knocked something over. There was a loud crash, but the old man didn't look up.

"Tata?"

Angelo and I turned and found ourselves looking at another man, this one younger than the first, though he also wore gold-rimmed glasses and had his thinning hair parted similarly on the side. Unlike the old man, this one was startled by our presence. Angelo moved closer to me and took my hand behind our backs.

"Chi sei?" asked the man, which sounded like "Kee say?" I'd picked up a little more Italian from Angelo and my time at the movies with him, so I knew he was asking who we were. But I was nervous and answered in English.

"Sorry," I said. "I'm sorry, we just . . ."

Even though I was speaking English, I still couldn't figure out what to say.

"You're Americans?" he responded in English. "What are you doing in here? How did you get in?"

"The gate, the doors . . . We were just . . ." My heart was beating so loudly in my chest I could barely hear myself speak.

"We know him," said Angelo, pointing to the old man. "I was in the hospital with him."

The younger man looked from us to the old man and back again. He seemed to squint at Angelo as if trying to focus or remember something. "You were the boy in the oxygen tent?"

Angelo nodded. "I'm Italian," he said, then pointed to me and added, "He's American."

"An Italian, an American, and a Pole walk into a bar," said the man.

Angelo and I just stared.

"I'm Polish," the man explained. "It's a joke. Sorry. I don't speak to many people anymore. My father was in the hospital because he had a small stroke."

"Sorry," I said.

"We saw him in the piazza," said Angelo. "And we wanted to say hello. We followed him . . ."

"He's not supposed to go outside by himself, but even when I lock up he manages to slip out. He also has dementia, so he's not always entirely sure where he is or what's going on. Come into the kitchen and sit. I'll make you some tea."

He led us through the apartment, down a short hallway to a small yellow kitchen.

"I'm Elijah," said the man. "Elijah Weiss. My father is Jakob."

"I'm Angelo, and this is Danny."

A deep thrill went through me because it was the first time anyone besides us had been told our new names. For Elijah and Jakob we were really truly named Angelo and Danny, and as far as they knew we had always been Angelo and Danny from the time we were born. Somehow having these strangers learn our names made it feel more official, and more . . . permanent.

"When did you come to Rome?" asked Angelo as we sat at a small wood table in the corner of the kitchen.

"During the war. We were refugees. I was just about your age, actually."

"That must have been scary," said Angelo, whose foot found mine under the kitchen table as we sat. Our legs pressed against each other, like we were keeping each other from disappearing.

"Yes, it was scary," said Elijah while he moved from the cabinets to the stove, putting water on for the tea and preparing some biscuits and cheese for us. "But we were placed in Cinecittà." He pronounced it "Chin-a-CHEE-ta."

"What's that?" I asked.

"It's a huge movie studio at the edge of Rome," Angelo answered.

"Correct," said Elijah. "I loved movies as a boy in Poland, and suddenly I was living where they were made. Of course we were in terrible squalor, and there was very little food. But we were housed in studio number five. Makeshift walls had been hammered together inside the huge soundstage, and there were hundreds and hundreds of others all around us. But for a boy of sixteen who loved cinema, it was a confusing wonderland. Half mad with grief because of the war, but astonished to find myself living in a place where movies were really made . . . It was an extraordinary time."

Elijah placed the biscuits and cheese in front of us, as well as empty teacups on little mismatched plates. "We scavenged through abandoned props and sets for furniture we could use to help our families. We found plaster columns and old carpets, and played among the scaffolding and fake stone walls."

"It was just you and your father?" I asked.

"Yes, but . . ."

"But what?"

"There were people from all over the world. Including a boy, around my age."

He looked at Angelo and me, and an expression I couldn't name passed across his face. It was like sadness, but also maybe hope and wonder. "We became friends."

We ate the cheese and biscuits and listened to the water rattling inside the heating teakettle.

"Sorry," he said. "I am speaking too much. As I said, I have not spoken to anyone in a long time besides my father and a few people behind the counter in shops."

"It's okay," I said, and Angelo agreed.

"The boy, your friend, was a refugee too," Angelo asked.

"Yes," said Elijah after a breath. "But he was from Germany. Also Jewish, but I spoke no German, and he spoke no Polish. Yet somehow we understood each other. I could tell he'd had a harder time in the war than me. It was visible in his eyes. I had my father but I believe he had no one with him. But when we were together, we didn't need words, and maybe because we couldn't speak, it was easier to not think about the past, and that meant all we had was right now."

Angelo's leg pressed harder against mine.

"There were so many places to explore," Elijah continued, "to hide, to build things. We made sculptures together in the trees, though maybe no one else would recognize them as sculptures. We made little cities out of rocks and buttons and whatever else we could find. Maybe in my friend's mind what we were making was very different from what I thought we were making, but the things themselves we never argued about or disagreed on. We just made things, or we'd race each other, and play catch with a ball we found, and we fashioned a bat from some wood and tried to see who could hit it farther, and everywhere, we'd wrestle.

"And all the while, on the other side of the camp, across a barbed wire fence we easily snuck through, movies were still being filmed. We'd watch together, amazed by the cameras and the costumes and the lights when they filmed at night. One day we were caught. But instead of getting in trouble, to our surprise they put us *in* the movie. Lots of refugees were used as extras, it turned out. You can still see us. A miracle in so many ways because . . ."

"Because what?" I asked.

"We didn't have long together."

"What happened?" asked Angelo.

Tears came to Elijah, and the teakettle started whistling. He turned off the heat and prepared the tea. "But there is always the movie."

"What was the name?" I asked.

"*Quo Vadis.*"

"I've seen it," said Angelo.

"I haven't," I said.

"It's about the fall of the Roman Empire. Nero goes mad and burns down the city," explained Elijah. "My friend and I are in an earlier scene, though—a happier one. We are in tunics, and brown capes that itched, listening to a speech in a big crowd. It was actually a little boring. We had to wait a lot, and we had to listen many, many times to the same speech. And it was so hot. We couldn't do anything. So at one point, between takes, I thought I'd teach him some Italian. The first words I tried were *ti amo.*"

I knew those words meant *I love you*, because people said it to each other all the time in the movies.

Unconsciously, I shot Angelo a quick glance, and he did the same toward me.

"I don't think he understood the words," said Elijah, "but maybe that's why I was brave enough to say them."

He took a breath and paused, and it felt like he was reliving the memory for a moment. And in another instant he had returned from Cinecittà to the present moment in his kitchen. "But you can still see us," he said. "Our backs are to the camera. First I turn, then Isak turns. That's my friend's name. Isak. And there we are. And there we remain. Like the poem."

Elijah poured the tea for us into our cups. It smelled of ginger and lemon.

"What poem?" I asked.

Elijah put down the teapot, raised a single finger, indicating *one moment*, then left the kitchen. Angelo's leg pressed against mine again, and our fingers found each other beneath the table. I was imagining Angelo in a tunic and brown cape. I found myself wondering if I should borrow my mother's camera, to take a picture of Angelo, but I couldn't quite imagine asking him to pose for me. In some weird way taking a picture would acknowledge that there was going to be a time when I couldn't just look at him, and maybe I didn't want to think about that. I could tell Angelo's mind was whirring as well, but neither of us said anything.

Elijah came back with a small, old book. He opened it and began turning through the pages, looking for something. As he searched, he said, "'Ode on a Grecian Urn'—do you know it?"

"'*Beauty is truth, truth beauty*,'" Angelo quoted. "John Keats."

I looked at Angelo, and thinking about our time on the grave made my cheeks flush. I didn't know if Elijah noticed, but he smiled and said, "Yes, that's the most famous line from the poem, but do you know the rest?"

Angelo shook his head.

"It's about two lovers painted on the side of a vase. And because they are frozen like that, they never grow old, and they never part. That's what film can do too, and I think of this whenever I see *Quo Vadis*. Do you know what *Quo Vadis* means?"

"No," I said.

"It's Latin," answered Elijah. "From the Bible. It means, *Where are you going?*" He then paused and repeated the phrase, almost to himself. "Where are you going?" He sighed, then continued. "In real life, no one can really answer that question. It's only people in poetry or books or movies, people who are going nowhere, who can be sure of their futures. Isak and I will always be sixteen, and together, for as long as the movie exists."

Elijah found what he was looking for in the old book. "Ah, here it is." Pointing to a line of poetry, he handed the book to me and I knew I was supposed to read it aloud, so I did. *"'More happy love!'"* I read, *"'more happy, happy love! For ever warm and still to be enjoy'd, For ever panting, and for ever young.'"*

Forever young, I thought.

Would I even really want that?

Would Angelo?

All children, except one, grow up—that's the beginning of *Peter Pan*. Of course lots of children don't grow up. But they don't fly off to Neverland. No, the children who don't grow up in real life are the ones who die, like in the movie we saw. *It's much better to grow up*, I thought. Even if you don't want to grow up, even if you don't know how you'll survive childhood, even if it seems like time is moving so slowly it will never happen . . . it will.

It must.

Angelo and I looked at each other. I watched the endless movements across his unmoving face—his eyelids blinking, his lips trembling slightly, loose strands of hair waving in the air, his chest rising and falling as he breathed.

We weren't figures on a vase, or a scene in a movie. No, right then we were real, and we did not know where we were going.

"I promised," came a raspy voice from behind us. "I promised I wouldn't tell the secret."

Standing in the door of the kitchen was the elderly Jakob Weiss, looking terrified and lost. He was pointing to the Keats book in my hand.

"I promised, and I never did. I never told their secret!"

Elijah quickly got up and went to his father, whispering something in Polish. With his arms around the older man, Elijah gently led him back to the big, crowded room. Angelo and I followed, and watched as Jakob was lovingly lowered into his reclining leather chair.

"Sorry," said Elijah. "I never know what he's going to say, or what language he's going to say it in. Sometimes it's Polish, sometimes Italian, but I suppose he heard us speaking in English."

I was still holding the Keats book, so I gave it back to Elijah.

"Keats was very important to him," said Elijah. "My father sold a lot of valuable Keats books to some friends of his, collectors who lived up the hill."

"The Monda brothers?" I asked, astonished.

Elijah appeared equally astonished. "You know of them?"

"My mom is working there for the summer. That's why I'm here."

"How funny," said Elijah. "I remember visiting them when I was younger. We went to their home, some of the very few visitors allowed in, from what my father told me. Tata was a sculptor who taught at a university nearby, but also a dealer in rare books and prints with two specialties: books by Keats and maps by Piranesi. Do you know who that is?"

I told him I didn't, though I figured Angelo knew the name, since Angelo seemed to know almost everything. Elijah led us over to a wide filing cabinet in the middle of the room and opened the drawers for us. Inside were detailed engravings of Italian landscapes, famous buildings like the Pantheon and the Colosseum, and dark, twisted interiors of shadowy prisons. There were sheets and sheets of architectural details, as if someone might shop for fireplaces or beams or ceiling decorations from these pages.

Then, in the last drawer, was a map of Rome I recognized immediately. It was the same map as the giant one on the wall in our secret room at the Monda Museum.

Jakob shifted in his chair and started speaking again. This time he spoke in a language I guessed was Polish. When we turned to look, he was cupping something in his palm, as if he wanted us to see it.

"Look!" said Angelo. "It's the plaster hand."

The old man beckoned Angelo and me over to him, and he transferred the small white object to our trembling hands.

"I want you to have this," he whispered. "Tell no one."

He turned from us and looked blankly out the window.

Elijah, who had been watching, dug up a small wood box. He wrapped the hand in a dusty piece of red velvet, and placed it inside.

"Keep it safe. My father really treasures it."

"Are you sure you don't want to keep it?" I asked.

"I'll tell you another secret," Elijah said. "Years ago, right as his dementia was setting in, he gave *me* the hand, saying the exact same words."

"Oh no," I said, pushing the box toward Elijah. "We can't take it! It's yours."

"No, no, this is even better. Now the hand isn't just a gift from my father, it's from me too."

"Are you sure?" I asked. Suddenly I wanted to tell this man my real name, to confide in him and show him that we trusted him as much as he trusted us. But how could I ask this when I didn't even know Angelo's real name myself?

Elijah smiled. It was clear his answer was yes.

"Do you know where it's from? Where your father got it?" Angelo asked.

"Not really, no," said Elijah. "He never said, but it was the one thing he wanted with him when he was in the hospital. He could barely speak, but he still managed to indicate he wanted the hand. I actually think it was given to him by his friends up the hill."

"The Monda brothers?"

"Well, one of them. After Vittorio died, Alberto asked my dad to carve the gravestone."

"The obelisk of books in the Non-Catholic Cemetery?" I asked.

"I can't believe you know it," said Elijah. "Tata hadn't done any carving for a while, but he did it as a favor for Alberto. Maybe the hand was a gift in exchange for the work. I don't know. But there definitely did seem to be a secret he wouldn't share with me."

"That's what your father was saying," said Angelo. "That he'd kept his secret."

"Yes, but . . . whatever he'd done, whatever story he'd been a part of . . . it's lost in the labyrinth of his mind. But there was clearly something that connected in his mind with me, and with you two."

The ginger lemon tea smelled clear and bright. There was so much I wanted to say, but I couldn't quite form the words. I wanted to say something about stories, and time, and how maybe stories don't really get lost, maybe they are just misplaced for a while. I wanted to say that we were in a city of excavations, where the past was constantly being dug up and rediscovered. Stones and statues and gold, wood and fabric and bones . . . aren't they all just the remnants of stories? But how in the world would I say that out loud? I couldn't find an answer, and I realized no one else had said anything for a long time either. So we sipped our tea, looked at the box between us, and welcomed the silence brought on by the little plaster hand.

THE HEAT OF YOUR BURNING SKIN

"There."

Angelo was pointing up toward the tall windows in the ornate facade of an old building on the opposite corner from the museum. "It was an eighteenth-century palazzo that was converted into apartments in the 1800s. If I lean out my bedroom window, we could see each other."

"You weren't kidding when you said you lived across the street from me," I said.

And then, to my shock, Angelo led me inside.

"This never happens," he said, "but I know everyone is out. Even my aunts. Come! We still need to be quick."

We raced through the lobby and up a wide, winding marble staircase to a set of large wood doors. Angelo took out a big metal key and let us into the apartment. The vestibule seemed bigger than the entire apartment where my mom and I were living. A dusty chandelier hung from a plaster rosette above us, and a wooden armoire stood hulking to the right. Its mirrored door was slightly open, and inside I could see an array of winter coats and boots that seemed like they were for another planet given how hot and sticky the air felt. I could hear flies buzzing from another room. Pork was roasting somewhere, and I could smell basil and garlic, and something else that seemed to me to be the smell of old rugs, or slowly rotting wood. It wasn't a bad smell, but it was strong. Angelo led me down a long twisting hallway lined with closed doors on either side until we came to the last door on the right, which had been painted blue a very long time ago.

"This was my mother's room when she was little," he said, "but now it's mine."

We stepped inside and he shut the door behind us. The room smelled like the rest of the apartment, dusty and old, but something was different, and I realized after a moment it was the smell of Angelo himself, vibrant and sweaty and alive. A rush ran through me as if my face was pressed against his neck, although at that moment I wasn't touching him at all. The room was large and an entire wall was lined with bookshelves, while the other three had dozens of old paintings hanging on them, as if he were living in an art gallery. We stepped onto a thick green area rug that lay in the middle of the wide wood floor like a field of grass, and I looked around. The first painting I really noticed was a large gold-framed picture of the Colosseum, like one we'd seen in an antique shop earlier. It was from the 1700s, when the building was covered in bushes and trees, with shepherds and sheep wandering around the inside. Then my eye caught smaller canvases of peasants and musicians, street scenes, and sunsets over Rome. Tacked directly into the wood paneling above the wrought iron headboard of his bed was a very old engraving that showed how to raise and lower an obelisk, with towers of scaffolding and hundreds of people using long ropes and huge winches. And taped to the empty spaces between many of the paintings were maps of the city, both antique and modern.

"Where did you get all these pictures?" I asked.

"Some have been in my family for a long time. Some I found at flea markets. Some are just posters and postcards I got in museums."

Beneath a large window at the far end of the room was a low table covered in little souvenir models of famous Roman places like the Vatican, the Trevi Fountain, and the Pantheon. Mixed among them were dozens of tourist snow globes with the names of Roman neighborhoods on them, and tiny plates of pasta or small Vespas inside. On his dresser were seedpods, dried leaves, sticks, and interesting stones that he'd collected around the city and lined up like a display in a museum.

We turned toward the wall opposite his bed, which was the one covered from floor to ceiling with books.

"My Roman library," said Angelo proudly.

I stepped closer and looked at the spines. The books were every shape and size, and they seemed evenly divided between English and Italian titles. As I looked from shelf to shelf, I could see history books, guidebooks, maps, and atlases, as well as collections of myths, short stories, novels, and photographic monographs of different areas and buildings around Rome. There was a huge section on Michelangelo and the Sistine Chapel, on the churches and the paintings of Caravaggio. There were children's books and textbooks and there were multiple copies of some titles. Books about the Tiber snaked across a single shelf like the river itself.

"Oh!" he said, as if he'd just remembered something.

He had a record player on a table by his bed. I thought about how much I'd like to have a record player, even though I loved my cassette deck very much. The problem was, I needed a permanent home to own a record player and records. I couldn't carry them with me in my bag from place to place. I watched a little jealously as Angelo flipped through his collection, which he kept in a couple of crates by his bed, until he found what he was looking for.

"You've played so much music for me," he said. "Now I'll play some for you." He slipped the record from its sleeve. "Remember when we were in the park under the umbrella pines? I told you about a piece of music." He put the record on the turntable and lowered the needle. "This is it. *Pines of Rome*."

We sat together on the floor at the foot of his bed, facing the wall of books. After a short crackle, a river of shimmering whistles and bells spilled out into the room. Then horns and woodwinds unfurled like the breeze through the leaves, and it was as if the trees themselves were calling to us and the sun was streaming down upon us and the smell of the earth was everywhere. We looked at each other as the music grew into a kind of joyous rapture. Then, unexpectedly, the music shifted. It moved into a low, quiet rumble, as if little children had been running through the pines, giggling and laughing, when suddenly they'd come upon something that made them stop in their tracks, something deep and mysterious they couldn't name, but could feel. Maybe it was a great green god of the forest, or the heartbeat of the earth itself, but I imagined the bare feet of the children taking in this ancient magic that existed beyond words.

"All these books," I said to Angelo as the thrum of the music rolled on. "You remember everything you read, don't you?"

"Yes, mostly. It just sticks."

As the sounds rose up again into a kind of rumbling storm cloud, I noticed a pile of VHS tapes on the floor. The titles I could see included *Roman Holiday*, *Three Coins in the Fountain*, *Spartacus*, something called *8½*, and his copy of *La Dolce Vita*. Angelo leaned down and pulled a tape from the pile.

Quo Vadis.

"We'll have to watch it," he said as cymbals crashed in the distance. "Do you think we'll be able to find Elijah and his friend?"

He looked into my eyes, and I had a feeling he'd never really shared any of this with anyone before. Sitting here, with his sweating body next to mine, the copy of *Quo Vadis* in his hand, I felt like I was being offered access to a treasure, and the treasure was Angelo. I suddenly understood why I was here. He needed me to witness all of this—his life, his library, his music, his interests—to wonder at everything, to consider them all worthwhile, and to love them.

And I did.

Deep in the middle of the night, as we lay shirtless and sweating, side by side on the blue nest in our secret room, Angelo and I were looking up at the big map. Earlier we'd circled Jakob and Elijah's home on the piazza in Trastevere, the very place this map itself may have come from. We weren't speaking very much, mostly because I was too distracted by thoughts of the calendar, and my mind wouldn't rest. Neither of us had a watch, though it felt like I could still hear the tick-tick-ticking of a clock somewhere. Or maybe it wasn't a clock. I'd read an interview once with a famous movie director who discussed the difference between surprise and suspense. *Surprise* is a boy on a bus and suddenly a bomb goes off. It's a jolt for one moment. But *suspense* is *knowing the whole time* there's a bomb on the bus, and watching the boy as he gets on and takes his seat, looks out the window at the passing city, listens to the people around him, maybe reads a book. Because the audience knows what's going to happen, it fills every moment with meaning and dread, because we're waiting for that terrible moment to come, in five . . . four . . . three . . . two . . . one . . .

"Danny?"

"Yes, Angelo?"

"Do you feel it?"

"Feel what?"

"I'm not sure exactly . . ."

The box with the hand was nearby. Angelo opened it and cradled the object gently, like it was a bird with a broken wing. "Do you think we'll really be able to find Elijah and his friend in *Quo Vadis*?" he asked me.

"I don't know. We'll try."

"Or . . ."

"Or what?"

"We can go to Cinecittà ourselves."

I laughed.

"I'm not joking, Danny. We can take my bike. It's no farther than the beach in Ostia. Just the other direction."

"Still . . ."

"I get these feelings sometimes," he said. "I'm not sure where they come from, but right now, I'm getting the feeling we need to . . ."

"What?"

"*Move.*"

I wasn't sure how to respond to him, because I'd had these sorts of feelings myself but didn't know how to talk about them. My hands were fidgety, so I pulled on the side of a nearby cardboard box that was part of the walls of our secret nest. Peeling back the flap, I found that the box was full of hundreds of the old brochures about the Monda Museum. I pulled one out and opened it.

"My mother told me she once saw Alberto Monda from my window," Angelo said. "When she was a little girl. Her parents had told her stories about their neighbor, and his collection of books by Keats. That's how she became interested in the poet. That's how I ended up—"

There was a long silence.

"Ended up what?" I asked. Angelo inhaled, and I could see he was making a decision about something. I felt my skin tingle though I wasn't sure why. I placed my hand on his hand, and waited for him to speak.

And then Angelo told me his story.

"My mom studied literature in college. She'd fallen in love with the poetry of Keats. She learned English so she could read his poems untranslated. After graduation she saved money and went to Britain for the first time. Keats died in Rome, but she wanted to visit the cities where he *lived*. She wanted to go on a kind of pilgrimage. She started in London, where he'd been born, and followed in his footsteps around England. She was eager to see a little seaside town called Margate, about a few hours north of London, because it was important to Keats. It's where he found peace, and became a writer.

"The inn where he stayed was still in business, run now by an older British man who once had wanted to be a poet himself. He'd never been married or had children. He and my mother fell in love. They got married and she moved to Margate, where she started working at the inn, and soon I was born."

"You were born in *England*?"

"Yes."

"You're English!"

"Technically I'm—"

"That's why your English is so good!"

"I'm Italian. Well, half. And my mother spoke Italian with me at home, so I've always been bilingual."

"How long did you live there?"

"Ten years."

"In Margate?"

"Yeah. I liked it there. It had seaside caves to explore, and an old amusement park called Dreamland. But something always seemed off. I thought it was because of my asthma, which was even worse there. I spent much time in the hospital. Because of this, I had very few friends. I was sick and lonely, and in much pain because of my chest. To distract myself, I read all the time. My mother gave me lots of books, but my favorite was a book about Roman mythology. I became obsessed with the stories, and the history of Rome. That's when I began collecting books about Rome, longing to go.

"The doctors in Margate were going to operate on my chest when I was ten because I was in so much pain, but my father died very suddenly, and my mother decided to come back home so her family could help raise me. My grandmother, aunt, uncle, and four cousins all lived in the building as well, so there were always people around.

"Soon after we got to Rome, I had the operation, in the same hospital you visited me in. As I recuperated at home for the summer, I read my books and watched every movie about Rome I could. Then, when the bandages were finally removed and my chest was healing, my mother took me on long tours of the city, and shared with me her favorite places. That's when I first saw for myself the Mouth of Truth, the elephant obelisk, and the Keats and Monda graves. She'd gotten a job as a manager in a fancy hotel in the city, and I started school in Rome for the first time, which was a difficult transition. But I loved it here. In Margate, like I said, I'd had the sense something was off, something was *missing*. I thought Rome was what I'd been missing. But now I realize I was wrong. Rome wasn't what I'd been missing."

"Oh," I said quietly. "What had you been missing?"

When his answer came, it came without any words at all.

As the night wore on and it was time for Angelo to leave, neither of us wanted to part. We stood together by our locked door, and struggled to dream up an excuse, any excuse, to stay together a little longer.

Finally, he thought of something to say. "What about the book your mom's been working on?"

"What about it?"

"Has she made any progress? I've been thinking about it."

"Yeah, I think so. She hasn't talked about it in a little while, but I can tell when her work is going well and when it isn't."

"Show me."

"Show you what?"

"The book. I want to see it."

"I can't do that. I'm sure it's locked up. And you need to get back."

"But you don't know if it's locked up? So maybe it isn't."

We found the book in the drawer where my mother kept it, as if it was waiting for us. I showed Angelo the amber pen and the rubber stamp from the de Furia Bookshop, then I put on the white gloves, opened the lid of the box, and took off the white paper wrap, revealing the yellowing cover of the book. I wasn't sure exactly what my mother had been doing to stabilize or clean the book exactly, but the patient looked to be in much better health now. The rich smell drew us closer.

"Open it," Angelo said.

I carefully opened the book and turned to the first page with writing. I explained to Angelo about the iron gall ink, and I told him about the surgical instruments she uses, the special lights, the magnifying glasses, and how she begins to decipher impossible text, the patterns she looks for, the ways she determines if a line was drawn above or below another, the ways in which the letters and the physical qualities of the ink and the paper and the thread and the binding can reveal an entire world.

Her red spiral-bound notebook was on the desk as well. I flipped through the pages. It was like seeing her brain working out the problems with the text, the language coming to her out of a thick haze. There were charts of letter shapes she'd drawn that looked like something from a code book, and her own attempts at copying the ancient Italian. As the notebook went on, longer groups of identifiable words began to appear. Where she wasn't entirely sure of a word, she'd placed it inside a set of parentheses, and where a word or phrase was completely missing, she'd used the three dots of an ellipsis. Eventually I found what looked like an entire deciphered and translated poem. Angelo read the Italian version to me, and I read the English one to him.

Il calor' della tua pelle ardente

L'oro dei tuoi occhi (lampeggianti)

(. . .) i miei (palmi) sfiorano le tue (coste)

(salendo) lungo la tua (schiena)

Come una (scalata) verso una vetta inesplorata

O un (incontro) con un dio vivente.

Mi stringo a te

Mentre il mare si agita e si gonfia.

Le onde si ergono

(Dure) contro la notte.

Infuria la tempesta

Ed io mi riverso, (rovinato),

sulla riva al tuo cospetto.

The heat of your burning skin

The gold of your (flashing) eyes

(. . .) my (palms) touch your (ribs)

(moving up) your (back)

like (climbing) an uncharted mountain

or (meeting) a living god.

I hold you tight

As the sea stirs and swells.

The waves are rising

(Hard) against the night.

The storm rages

And I am washed up, (wrecked),

beside you on the shore.

And then there was only our breathing, and our two bodies beside each other, and our fingertips touching beneath the notebook, and the hair of our arms trembling and brushing, and we didn't move for a long time. We were wrecked beside each other on the shore. The words were my words, written in my voice, about my feelings for Angelo, and his for me, or at least that's how it felt. Maybe it was just the intensity of what was happening between us, that *whatever* poems we read, like the music we listened to or the movies we watched, would have felt like they were meant just for us.

"Don't you understand, Danny?" Angelo asked.

"Understand what?"

He picked up the fragile, old book. "This is it."

"This is what?"

"The writing I was telling you about, on the ship. It's the love poems written by Dante Ferrata, for the elephant, and the sailor."

"But . . . that's not possible."

"In stories, anything is possible."

"My mother said the book has no author name, no actual date."

"I know."

"No person, or elephant, is identified as the object of love in the poems!"

"I know. But I'm sure of it. Can't you feel it? Giovanni bound this book with the poems Dante wrote on the ship."

"Angelo, you're making all this up."

"Take me to the Mouth of Truth."

I stared into his unblinking eyes and sighed. I took the book from him. "But you said Giovanni couldn't read the poems."

"No. He was illiterate."

"I don't like that, Angelo. It's too sad."

"I can't change the story."

"Well, that hurts too much to think about."

"You must learn to bear the pain."

"Is that the point of the story? To learn to bear the pain?"

"I don't know," he said. "But it's not over yet."

"What's not over?"

"The story of Dante and Giovanni."

"But they died hundreds of years ago."

"I mean there is more to their story."

"There's more?"

"There's always more."

"So tell me!"

"Maybe I'll tell you if—"

I'm not sure which of us heard it first, but the sound of footsteps was echoing down the hallway.

"Hide!" I whispered to Angelo, who looked left, then right, then slipped behind the door.

My mother entered. I spun around with the book still in my hands. She stared at me like she was hallucinating, then she shook her head slightly and said, "At least you're wearing gloves."

"I'm sorry, Mom."

"What in the world are you doing? Were you talking to someone?"

Behind her, I could see Angelo's elbow sticking out from behind the door. It was so dark that even if she turned around she probably wouldn't see it, but my heart was racing and my hands shook. "I was just thinking about the book, and couldn't sleep. I was trying to read it out loud."

"I'm glad the book intrigues you, but this is very irresponsible of you."

"I know."

"You shouldn't be here without a grown-up. Especially not at two in the morning."

She took the book from me and I noticed she seemed to check something inside the front cover before she wrapped the book in the paper and placed it inside the box. After she returned it to the drawer by her desk, I turned off the lamp and maneuvered myself so she had to leave the room first. As I closed the door, I stuck my head back inside, as if I was taking one last look. I got a glimpse of Angelo still pressed into the corner of the room behind the door.

Our eyes met. He raised his eyebrows, and I understood that he meant *I'll be fine.*

I quietly shut the door.

THE EYE OF GOD

The spaceship was waiting for us, just beyond the dark trees. We walked down the gravel road, past a shadowy Egyptian temple, and came to the edge of the silver lagoon, where a fully rigged pirate ship floated in the moonlight. We'd run away, and ended up in a fairy-tale kingdom where dreams were built from wood and canvas and plaster.

We'd ridden to the edge of town where the movie studio stood, hiding Angelo's motorbike in the bushes across from the main gate, where the word *Cinecittà* was spelled out in silver letters over the gated entrance. Then we'd circled the grounds until we found a wall low enough for us to shimmy over.

Angelo had planned it all, of course.

We'd spent the last five days together, nearly nonstop. Our time was filled with more wandering and food, coffees and sandwiches, and legs rubbing slowly against each other beneath café tables. In the evenings we wanted to watch the movies he had on VHS, and because it was so hard to sneak me into his house, he decided to sneak his television and video player *out* one morning. We set them up in our secret room after hunting for a half hour to find a working outlet. Lying side by side, we quickly discovered it was nearly impossible to get all the way through an entire movie without our bodies demanding we take long breaks. But eventually, amid the sweat and the sheets, our attention would return to the little black-and-white screen, where we watched as chariots raced and an Egyptian queen arrived in Rome at the end of a procession made up of what looked like a million people, and a big-eyed girl with a romantic secret ran away with a handsome man on the back of a motorbike that looked just like Angelo's.

Finally, we watched *Quo Vadis*. The movie is three hours long—though it took us much longer than that to watch the whole thing. We eventually found what we were looking for—a scene set on the side of a mountain as someone gives a speech to a large gathering of people in tunics and capes, and just as Elijah had described, two boys about our age can be seen next to each other. First one turns to listen, and then the other, and we knew it had to be them, it had to be Elijah and Isak.

After that, Angelo immediately hatched the plan that brought us here, beneath the long, moonlit shadow of the spaceship. He took my hand and led me down a medieval European street, until he pulled me through a saloon door into the Wild West. A few workmen could be seen in the distance pushing trollies with large wood boxes, but luckily it was very late when we'd snuck in and there were few people around.

It was scary following Angelo in silence through the darkness of the lot, between the huge buildings and old props from films, which were scattered everywhere like remnants from a society of giants. I tried to imagine what it was like for Elijah and Isak to find themselves living here, ripped away from everything they'd ever known with only their friendship to sustain them. I tried to pretend Angelo and I were the two of them, exploring this place alone at night, stepping past a gold carriage parked on a lawn, a huge hand rising from a parking lot pointing to the sky, and the monolithic head of a king buried up to its eyes.

I was nervous, but the feel of Angelo's hand in mine was as reassuring as it always was. Every corner brought some new bit of magic or hidden delight. We came upon a huge barnlike metal structure with a giant number five painted high above us and a small sign by the locked doors that listed the titles of films that had been made inside, many of which we'd watched on Angelo's VHS tapes: *Ben-Hur, Cleopatra, Roman Holiday,* and, to our delight, *Quo Vadis.* We walked around to the other side and found a huge garage-like door wide open. The sets for these movies were, of course, long gone. Inside at the moment was a vast golden palace, sparkling as if it had been snipped from the illustrations of a book and transported whole to this imposing space. We would have explored further, but even at this hour, there were men working, moving a grid of metal pipes into the air. So, we slipped back down the dark roads until we stumbled upon a stone gate framed by concrete eagles with their wings spread. Curious, we climbed into the enclosure and discovered empty cages of all sizes.

"For the animals they use in the movies, I guess," said Angelo quietly. We heard a low rumble in the night, which we followed through the abandoned iron maze, and to our shock there was a living occupant being held captive in the zoo.

Standing there, not twenty feet from us, on the other side of the rusted metal bars, was an elephant.

An actual *elephant*, as tall and still as a house.

We stared in shock, and for a moment it felt like time had

collapsed, and any moment Dante Ferrata would appear to welcome us, awestruck, into the seventeenth century.

Angelo pointed to a sign written on a small board outside the cage: *Intervista, F. Fellini.*

"Fellini," he said. "He directed *La Dolce Vita*. The elephant must be for a new movie he's making here."

With Angelo beside me, I felt something shift in the air, as if we'd suddenly fallen into a different story, one where a spell was cast and we'd been *summoned* by this extraordinary creature. Staring in wonder, the elephant didn't seem like an animal at all. I thought of the poem my mom had translated . . .

> *like climbing an uncharted mountain*
> *or meeting a living god*

Neither Angelo nor I could speak.

Everything he had described when Dante met the elephant was true. It was the strangest sensation, as if the elephant *knew* us somehow, like we were all the *same person*.

I wanted to let the elephant out of the cage, to free her, but where would she go? Would she walk down the long highway and wander through the side streets of Rome, forever trying to get back home? Where *was* her original home? I read somewhere that the ears of an African elephant are shaped like Africa, and the ears of an Indian elephant are shaped like India, but I couldn't get a good look at her ears. How had she gotten here?

Then, with an unexpected grace, the elephant began to move. She glided forward, her feet stepping silently into the dirt as she traversed the enclosure. Stopping inches from us, she raised her trunk between the bars, as if she wanted to greet us. Angelo stepped behind me and pressed against me so our bodies became a single body, and he slid his hand into mine, so our hands became a single hand with ten fingertips. Angelo's breath was in my ear, and his body was at my back, and we reached our hand forward. We touched the elephant.

The end of her trunk delicately explored our hand. She was surprisingly warm and soft. I had the sense she was trying to communicate, but I wasn't sure if she was asking us a question or trying to tell us a secret. I wondered if Angelo was thinking what I was thinking—that no matter how hard we tried, we'd never really know what she was thinking. In fact, I felt sure no human would ever fully understand what an elephant was thinking. Not really. Not even Dante Ferrata. But I fully understood how someone could fall in love with this creature, how meeting one of these mysterious beasts could make you reassess your life, your values, your dreams, your future. I was sure that's what was happening to me at that moment, though there was only the sound of the workmen in the distance, and Angelo's breathing in my ears.

The elephant turned her giant head so one of her black eyes could look at us more clearly. Surprisingly, her eye wasn't much larger than a person's eye, yet there was something uncanny about it. Perhaps because it was set into such a vast sea of gray skin, it hovered on the side of her face like a lonely planet seen in the distance, or the center of a swirling hurricane in the ocean. Somehow it was terrifying and enthralling, like the oculus in the Pantheon, or the eye of God. She gently withdrew her trunk.

Angelo and I slid apart, separating like cells under a microscope.

For some unknown reason I started to cry, and when I turned to face Angelo, I saw there were tears in his eyes as well.

The stars had been obliterated by a dark covering of clouds, and the motorbike's little headlight must have looked like a firefly to the passing vehicles, if they even noticed it at all. The engine roared in our ears and the wind whipped mercilessly against us as the temperature dropped. It was impossible to speak while we were on the bike, but that was fine because we both understood we shouldn't talk about what had just happened to us with the elephant. The experience needed to exist in a space beyond language right now. So we rattled down the highway, alone in our thoughts, our bodies clinging together for safety as we bumped and flew back toward Rome, the streetlamps flashing by.

THE PLASTER HAND

I was slowly, carefully tracing the scar across Angelo's chest with the tip of my finger. His skin was gold in the candlelight, and his breathing was audible but steady. We stayed like that for a long time, just the sound of air going in and out of his lungs as he concentrated on the sensation. I knew it was still intense and challenging for him to be touched like this, and he kept his eyes closed, but he said it felt good and was helping him heal. I was struck by how translucent his eyelids were, how I could detect the movement of his eyes beneath the thin pink lids.

He opened his eyes and said, "I have more to tell you about Dante and Giovanni."

We shifted positions. He leaned up on his elbow and I moved down so he could whisper into my ear as his fingertips drifted up and down my side. "The sculptor remained employed by his master for many years," he said. "Eventually, Bernini was commissioned to create a series of standing angels for an ancient bridge that spanned the Tiber River. Dante was told to design all the angels and then build a model of the entire thing to share with the pope, who had commissioned him. Dante always preferred to carve directly into marble, but he began creating the model from wood and clay before casting it all in plaster. As he worked on the very first angel, he found himself consumed by a kind of vision. His fingers worked the dark red clay, and from beneath his touch there appeared a face and a body that seemed strangely familiar, yet he could not say why.

"It was only after casting the figure in plaster and setting the three-foot-tall gleaming white angel on the small wooden bridge that Dante realized, quite by accident, he'd made a likeness of his lost sailor friend Giovanni.

"Unwanted tears came to Dante's eyes, and without thinking, his hand reached out and grabbed on to one of the angel's hands. A sudden cascade of visions and memories flooded Dante's mind, and these images were so bright and vivid that he felt like he'd fallen into a dream. He saw Giovanni on the ship, and naked in his cabin lit by lantern light, and standing against the sunset with the wind in his hair. In a blinding flash he saw him standing before him in Bernini's studio, pleading with him to take the bound book made from his shipboard love poems. A loud sound, like a hard snap, brought Dante back to the reality of the studio, and when he looked down he discovered he'd accidentally broken off the statue's hand. Staring at the small white object, Dante heard the door to the studio open. Instinctively, he slipped the plaster hand into his pocket and ran from the dusty room.

"In all the years since the elephant obelisk had been completed, Dante had never allowed himself to walk near it, but that night, as he fled from the studio, he made a detour. Looking up at the monument as it glowed blue in the moonlight, an immeasurable sadness overwhelmed him. Dante reached into his pocket, where his fingers gripped the small white hand of Giovanni, and he found himself reliving the awful moments as the ship docked in Italy. He saw Giovanni pushed overboard and the terror in the eyes of his beloved elephant in the moments before she was killed by the captain. A pain ran through his body thinking about how there had been no proper burial for the elephant, no leaves, no dust. What had become of her body? Perhaps she'd been donated to a science museum or medical school, or perhaps she had simply been dropped into the sea. He called up to the carved marble elephant and begged her forgiveness, though he wasn't sure if he spoke out loud or only in his mind. He remembered the visions he had soon after the accident, visions of her ghost wandering the streets of Rome. Was she still wandering them, all alone? *What can I do?* he asked. *What can I do?*

"Then an answer took root in his mind, and he found himself running to the edge of the river, where he gathered up handfuls of dirt and stray leaves. When his pockets were full, he rushed back to the plaza, climbed up the stone base, and rubbed the dirt from his pockets onto the elephant as best he could, blowing the leaves over the elephant's head. He almost didn't hear the shouts from below, and by the time he looked down, a small crowd had gathered, thinking he was a madman trying to deface the sculpture that all of Rome had come to love, not knowing he himself had carved it. In the distance he saw more people heading toward him, alerted by the noises of the crowd, and with a terrified leap he landed on the paving stones and ran off down a long, narrow street before anyone could stop him.

"Walking alone through the twisting streets of the city, he watched as a fog gathered ahead of him, and within a few moments the mist had taken a familiar shape. It was easy to imagine the ghostly presence of his elephant floating ahead of him, gliding between the leaning stone walls of the buildings on either side of the street. He followed it into a large open plaza, where the ghostly shape rose up and dissolved into the night sky. Dante began to weep, believing the soul of his elephant had finally been released. He wiped the tears from his eyes, and realized he didn't know where he was. But on the other side of the moonlit plaza he saw the wide empty expanse of the Piazza di Spagna, and between him and the piazza were the gurgling waters of the Fountain of the Broken Boat.

"A dark figure stood like the shadow of death at the base of the fountain. Dante, worried he was going mad, covered his eyes. He'd heard rumors of a figure called the Shadow of the Boat who haunted the fountain, but he'd been sure the stories were invented by locals to scare the tourists. But when he looked again, the shadow had loosed itself from the boat and begun to move toward him with its arm extended. Dante wondered if this was how Death was going to take him, heartbroken and alone in the middle of the night. Not sure what else to do, when the figure was within reach, he felt compelled to place the small white plaster hand into the upturned palm of the dark figure, a small hand within a larger hand, like an offering, a payment for more time.

"The figure paused for a moment, then lowered its hood, revealing the glowing face of Giovanni Argento.

"After that, no one knows exactly what happened. Some believe the two of them made their way to an island, or somewhere secret by the sea, where Giovanni could make his living on the water. It's easy to imagine Dante's joy, living alone with Giovanni and freed from Bernini's control, where now he could carve only what he wanted to carve. Perhaps the one thing he wanted to carve was Giovanni's likeness.

"Without access to marble, maybe he started using the endless supply of sand that ran beneath their feet along the shore. His sculpted visions of Giovanni would rise each day until the tide would come at night, returning the glistening bodies to the sea.

"Over time, with much patience, maybe Dante taught Giovanni to read. And if he did, do you know what I think the first words he read on his own were?"

I did know.

"*Ti amo,*" I said as an electric shiver ran through my body. I pulled myself closer to Angelo, who didn't look away from me.

"Many years later," he continued, "after both men had died, maybe the only things they left behind were the plaster hand and the bound book of love poems Giovanni had hopefully been able to finally read. The book and the little plaster hand somehow made their way to the Mondas. Then the hand went from Alberto to Jakob."

"And now it's ours," I said.

"Yes."

I should have been satisfied with that, but I wasn't. I wanted to know more. I always wanted to know more, especially when the ticking of the bomb was getting so loud. "You really don't know what happened to them?"

"I said already. No one does."

"But . . . they were happy, right?" And somehow I wasn't just asking about Dante and Giovanni. I was asking about me and Angelo, and maybe everyone else who'd ever fall in love. I wanted assurance. I wanted proof, or a promise, that everything was going to be alright. But who can offer that proof or make that promise? I was old enough to understand that life didn't come with guarantees. But without them, what was left? Only hope, I supposed, and trust, and faith. And the love itself, which needed to be protected and treasured.

I looked at Angelo. *What about us?* I asked him without words.

And silently he answered, *I don't know.*

BURN AFTER READING

From one corner of my mother's lab, I watched as she packed everything. She polished and cleaned the instruments she'd brought with her and slid them into their specially made cases. She filed, folded, or threw out what seemed like an endless amount of paper. She collected her pens and notebooks, and separated her own books from the ones she needed to return to the reference library downstairs. It was unbelievably hot and we were both sweating. Angelo's mother needed him for something, I wasn't sure what, and it was the first day in a long while we hadn't spent together. I'd soaked a rag in cold water and placed it on my head, but it still felt like I was going to melt. The backs of my thighs stuck to the leather seat, and my fingers rubbed the smooth brass nailheads that outlined the chair.

"Are you sad we're leaving?" Mom asked as she continued to pack. I didn't answer, and she quickly turned around to look at me. I caught her eye and smiled a little, but still didn't say anything.

"You've had a good summer?"

I nodded.

"I remember missing the food last time we left," she said, returning her focus to the papers on the desk. "When we got back to the States, it seemed like nothing tasted as good as it did when we were here."

"I like the strawberries," I said, but I wasn't thinking of the strawberries.

"Do you think you'll want to come back?"

"To Rome?"

"To Rome."

"How could I do that?"

"I don't know," she said. "But would you want to?"

I couldn't bear it anymore and began to cry. I tried to keep it quiet, but my mother heard and looked at me as I was wiping my eyes.

"What if I stayed?" I asked. "What if I didn't leave?"

My mother paused. "So you had a good time, I guess."

I didn't answer.

"You're serious," she said.

"Yes."

"What about school?" she asked me, with a gentleness in her voice that surprised me. "And where would you live? You can't stay at the Monda. When the summer ends the place is going to be full again."

"There's an American boarding school. I could live there."

"With whose money?"

"I'll save up," I said. "I'll get a scholarship."

"Come here," said my mother. "There's something I want to show you."

When I joined her at the desk, the only thing still out was the old book. She let me slip on her white gloves and open it one last time. I leaned over to smell the paper again. I wondered why the smell of books was always so powerful. Maybe it was because it's what we imagine time itself might smell like. I tried to picture a man named Dante Ferrata, late at night on a ship, writing these very words on this actual paper, from a glass bottle of brown ink he'd brought with him in his bags. I tried to imagine the flickering lantern light, the rocking of the ship, the distant moans of the elephant, the young sailor circling him, waiting outside his door, finally being invited in. The way that—

"You weren't alone, were you?" said my mom. "When I found you in here that night?"

I didn't know what to say as the vision of Dante and Giovanni slipped away.

"Was it the boy across the street?"

My heart started to pound. I couldn't speak. I looked away.

"Michael," my mother said quietly as she touched me on the shoulder. "Talk to me."

Michael.

Who was Michael?

I had been *Danny* for so long now that it startled me when my mother said my real name. It was as if the name was no longer mine.

"I've seen you together," she said.

I put the book down on the desk to calm myself as she paused. I could hear my blood rushing in my ears.

"You'll miss him," she said after a moment. I noticed it wasn't a question. Dante and Giovanni came to my mind, perhaps as a way to avoid talking about "the boy across the street." Maybe I'd distract her by asking about the sculptor and the sailor. My mother and I could start going to libraries and archives, and I would find out if they were real, and I'd solve the mystery of the book for my mother and the world, all without talking about Angelo.

But I couldn't do that. The idea of actually saying Dante's and Giovanni's names out loud to her at this moment, and trying to explain the whole story, and then looking for actual proof, all seemed impossible, and wrong, like it would be a betrayal of Angelo. Dante and Giovanni belonged to Angelo and me, and I felt they shouldn't be shared. Not yet, anyway. But what should I do? I was so shocked my mother knew about Angelo, and her voice had been calm when she'd spoken.

"We were curious about who wrote the poems."

"You and everyone else," she said with a little laugh. "That reminds me. I did come upon something interesting I wanted to tell you about before we left."

"What?"

"About two months ago, right after I first showed you the book, I discovered a corner of the endpaper was loose. So I got my scalpel and my lifting spatula and started peeling it back. It turned out the endpaper wasn't actually the endpaper. Rather it was the first page of the book that someone had glued down over the original endpaper. When I caught you in my office, I wondered if you'd found it."

I suddenly had a vague memory of my mother glancing inside the front cover that night as she put the book away.

"Why was it glued down?" I asked.

"That was my first question. When I pulled back the page, I found . . ."

"What?"

"This."

She handed me a small yellow piece of paper that had been folded in half. On the outside it said, *Dopo averlo letto, brucialo.*

My Italian had improved, but I didn't recognize all the words.

"What does that mean?" I asked.

"Burn after reading."

I unfolded the card and looked at the words inside, written in blue ink.

Per Alberto de Falco. Ti amo.

I could translate these words myself.

For Alberto de Falco. I love you.

"Who is Alberto de Falco?"

"That was my question as well," said my mother. "But I couldn't stop thinking about why a person would hide a little note in a book, and then hide the book, pen, and rubber stamp behind a panel in the wall. It seemed like someone was trying very hard to keep a secret."

"Why?"

"That's what I wanted to know. So I did some digging."

I leaned in closer.

"I began with the rubber stamp that said *Libreria de Furia.* It took some time, but I tracked the shop down to a very small town outside of Naples in the south of Italy. I was lucky and someone miraculously answered the phone at the library there. I was then able to access the genealogy records, births, deaths, things like that, which eventually led me to the local papers, where I was guided to an interesting article from 1916. The librarian xeroxed it and mailed it to me, and it finally arrived a few days ago."

"What does it say?"

My mother reached into a drawer and handed the paper to me. The headline, translated from Italian, said, *Two Young Men Vanish.*

I finished the article and looked up at my mother, my heart beating hard. "What is this?" I asked.

"Their secret," she answered, and all I could think of was Angelo.

RUN AWAY WITH ME

The bell rang above the door of the Libreria de Furia as the young man entered the tiny shop. It was the third time he'd been in that week, and he worried someone would notice. Of course there was one person he hoped would notice, but that made him too nervous to speak. He knew he should stay away because there could only be danger and grief if he went into the bookshop too often, but he couldn't help himself. He went back. And there, at the far end of the shop, behind the counter, near a stack of dusty books, was the reason he couldn't sleep, the reason he kept coming back again and again.

The young clerk had looked up when the bell rang, as he always did. A few books had disappeared recently from the shelves, so he had to keep an eye on who was in the store, even though everyone in town knew one another. And he knew the person who had walked in. He was the son of the newspaper printer from down the street. They'd been in school together when they were younger, but they'd both left to work for their fathers. This had to be the third or fourth time he'd come into the shop this week. He never spoke; he just looked around and left. If anyone else had behaved like that, he'd have been the prime suspect for the recent thefts, but there was something about this young man that made the clerk feel there were other reasons he was in the store. He just couldn't figure out what they might be. For some reason, these mysterious visits from his former classmate made him nervous, and his beating heart would keep him from initiating a conversation, which was especially odd because everyone spoke to everyone in town.

The clerk was feeling brave this particular day, though, and after his former classmate had browsed for a few minutes, he stepped out from behind the counter and walked across the shop.

"Alberto," he said, "I've seen you in here a few times this week. Is there a book I can help you find?"

Alberto jumped a little because he was so nervous, but he calmed himself and said, "Hello, Vittorio. I . . . I am not sure what I am looking for." But that was not true. He knew exactly what he was looking for, and he was face-to-face with him right now. Alberto thought Vittorio bristled with a kind of thrilling energy, even when the clerk was standing still.

"I remember we sat near each other at school because everything was alphabetical," said Vittorio. "Alberto de Falco and Vittorio de Furia. You liked puzzles. You were always creating little games and secret codes. Do you still do that?"

Alberto was shocked Vittorio remembered him at all. He did still love games and puzzles, but he was so nervous he couldn't figure out what to say, until he noticed the small book in the clerk's hand.

"What's that?"

"Oh, this?" said Vittorio. "It's an English poet I've been reading."

"You speak English?"

"No, it's translated into Italian."

"I've never read poetry," said Alberto. "May I see the book?"

As the object passed from one hand to the other, Alberto felt Vittorio's fingertips for just a fraction of a second, enough to send a rush through his entire body. Shaking, he looked at the blue cloth cover, then opened the book.

"Poetry is best when read out loud," said Vittorio.

"Oh."

"Pick a poem."

Alberto found a page, and Vittorio moved so he was standing beside him. Vittorio's fingers were stained black with ink, and he suddenly felt self-conscious. "I stamp the books we acquire with the name of the shop," he shyly explained. "The ink gets all over my hands and I have to be careful not to ruin the books."

Alberto laughed. "I work at my father's printing press. I am always covered in ink."

The heat from Vittorio's body radiated like the sun, and he placed his hand so it seemed as if he was helping to cradle the book, but what he was actually cradling was Alberto's hand. He read the poem, and as the images appeared—two running lovers, a frozen forest, a Grecian urn— it felt as if they were being welded forever into the metal of his mind.

Alberto and Vittorio began spending all their time together. They'd wait for each other after work, and they'd go for long walks alone to the edge of town, or they'd sit by the small piazza laughing secretly to each other. Sometimes they'd disappear for hours down empty lanes and into falling-down barns on abandoned farms.

It didn't take long for people to notice. At first there was pleasure that the young men had each found a friend, since both had been such loners. But stories began to circulate, first among the old ladies who gathered in the church doorways, then spreading wider, like poison in the roots of a tree. No one knew why they were bothered so much by the sight of the two young men walking so tightly together. Maybe it was the way they whispered, the way they were seen at night in the bell tower or emerging from back doorways in the mornings. Something about their closeness caused *alarm, and their families grew worried. Young women were brought by their homes for them to meet, and while the conversations were always pleasant, neither young man seemed interested in marriage. A fortune teller who lived at the end of a lonely road was consulted by their mothers, but all she could see in her visions were two locks and a single bed, which seemed like a terrible omen.*

What they came to call the crazy idea had been Vittorio's. "Run away with me," he'd whispered one night into Alberto's ear as they lay side by side on the thick grass of a small hill outside of town where they bicycled sometimes to be alone. Alberto laughed, thinking he must be kidding, but Vittorio, who wasn't even sure why he'd said it, didn't blink. The idea had just come into his mind like an impossible dream or wish, but moments after the words had been spoken out loud, both young men knew what they were going to do. Alberto wasn't sure he could bear the pain it would cause his mother, but it was clear there was no other way, so they started planning.

In the bookshop, they scoured dictionaries and finally picked their new last name. The word they chose was an imperative verb, which meant cleanse *or* purify, *and that seemed perfect for two people who were going to take action and begin again. They would have a clean start with a pure name.*

Monda.

They would become Vittorio and Alberto Monda.

In fact, everything would be pure when they arrived in their new city with their new story. No one would question them, no one would bother them, and no one from their past would ever be able to find them or stop them.

They were both about the same height, with the same-colored hair and eyes, and they would grow the same mustache to make the story even more believable. They had managed to save some money, and for them moving day was filled with the joy and terror of what was to come, and also the grief of everything and everyone they were leaving behind. On his last night at home, Alberto kissed his mother good night and hugged her for so long that she said, "What's gotten into you? You're squeezing the life out of me."

"I wish I could make you happy," he said.

"So fall in love and get married, already," she answered.

Mama, Alberto thought to himself. Please forgive me.

Alberto and Vittorio left under the cover of darkness. They had sworn they would only bring the clothes and food they needed, but they discovered later that each of them had hidden a single object that would help them remember the past they were leaving behind. Alberto brought an amber fountain pen his mother had given him, which had once belonged to his beloved grandfather, and Vittorio took the little rubber stamp with the name of his father's bookshop. They traveled from the tiny town of their birth without stopping for two full days, eating the food they'd packed, and when they felt safe, they rested at the next inn they found. It was thrilling to tell the clerk their new names, to say they were brothers, and to be shown a room with two locks and a single bed, which seemed like a wonderful omen.

The two of them traveled for months, moving from town to town, visiting all the bookshops they passed along the way. They began finding rare volumes, which they bought for very little money and later resold at great profits. Their eye for special books and their skill as businessmen *quickly sharpened, and by the time they got to Rome, they had enough cash to purchase a falling-down palazzo at the top of the Janiculum Hill. To the unwelcoming world they were eccentric brothers who loved English poetry and demanded to be left alone. But in their book-lined home they finally had the space to be what they really were: two young people in love.*

Every year they celebrated the anniversary of the night they arrived in Rome with a glass of wine by the fire. On their tenth anniversary, Vittorio decided to do something different. In a local market he'd come across an old book with indecipherable writing. The binding had fallen off, and the parchment and board covers were rotting, but it had just the sort of code Alberto would love to try to solve. So he decided to present it as a special gift.

In all the time that had passed since they'd left their village, neither of them had ever written down a single thing that could give away their secret. There were no love letters, no little notes, no diaries, no missives home, nothing. But Vittorio suddenly felt compelled to write their secret down, to commit it to paper and give it to Alberto. So on a small yellow card, with Alberto's amber pen, he wrote the words. He felt nervous as he formed the letters. It felt subversive and full of danger to have this physical evidence in his handwriting.

Per Alberto de Falco. Ti amo.

Knowing the risk he was taking, Vittorio wrote on the front of the card.

Dopo averlo letto, brucialo.

Perhaps he meant it as a joke, but he wasn't really joking. He wanted the book saved, and the card burned.

Alberto read the card. It seemed to vibrate in his hands, and he wept.

"Vittorio, you shouldn't have written it down."

"I was going to try to make up a code," said Vittorio, "but I'm not good at that sort of thing."

Alberto opened the book and was delighted to discover the impossible writing.

"Maybe that's enough of a puzzle for you," said Vittorio. "Let me know if you figure out what it says."

They fell into each other's arms.

Later, when Alberto brought the little card to the fire, he couldn't bear to commit Vittorio's love to the flames. So, one afternoon when he was alone in the house, he took the folded paper and glued it safely inside the front cover of the book, where he trusted its message would remain safe from prying eyes. Many years passed, and long after Vittorio had died, and after Alberto had shared his secret with his friend Elijah Weiss so Elijah could carve a grave of books meant for him and his beloved, and after he gave Elijah the little plaster hand as a token of his gratitude, and after Alberto had saved the books of Florence, and after he had been diagnosed with his final illness, Alberto held the special gift Vittorio had given him and wondered what would become of the book in the future. He'd never been able to crack the code, but more important, glued beneath the first page of the book was the only message of love ever recorded between the two men. He couldn't destroy the book, or sell it, or risk someone finding it, so he hid it away as best he could, along with the amber pen and the rubber stamp. He placed them under a pile of documents, at the end of a shelf, behind a false panel, surrounded by shadows, somewhere in his vast palace made of books.

After Alberto died, Elijah became too ill to carve the final digits into the year of Alberto's death, and that is why the second year remains *uncarved on the obelisk of books in the Non-Catholic Cemetery, to this very day.*

I had never seen Angelo's handwriting before, and the pages he'd written for me trembled in my hands. I stared at him in wonder. Yesterday I'd shared with him what my mother had discovered: in 1916, Alberto de Falco, the son of the local newspaper printer, and Vittorio de Furia, the son of the local bookshop owner, had disappeared from their small town in southern Italy. The Mondas were not, in fact, brothers. They were two young men who had left everything they'd known so they could be together. That's all we really knew, but Angelo had spent the night writing their love story for me, and now it belonged to the two of us.

He reached over and removed the small plaster hand from its box. He held it in the glow of the candle, turning it slowly. The little object cast a huge shadow on the opposite wall, and I thought there was something appropriate about this tiny thing casting such a large shadow over me and Angelo.

"What are we going to do with the hand when it's time for me to go?" I asked. "It doesn't feel right for me to take it back to America."

"And it doesn't feel right for me to keep it in Rome without you."

My mind spun, but then an idea hit me.

"I know what we should do," I said.

Vee meowed and leapt into the shadows as I explained my plan to Angelo. I folded the pages he'd given me and hid them carefully beneath the blue nest. We stood and put on our shirts. I found my glasses, adjusted them, and we headed out into the dark city. We walked swiftly along the river toward Testaccio and the Non-Catholic Cemetery. The night was very dark, as the clouds kept obscuring the moon, and many of the streetlamps were broken. The sense of menace in the air was particularly strong. Dogs barked, something screeched, and in the distance we thought we heard someone scream.

We walked along the river, then crossed the Ponte Sublicio and found the hole in the fence where we snuck into the cemetery. The Mondas' marble grave was silhouetted in the darkness, and it drew us like a beacon, a lighthouse with no light. Angelo held the wood box with the plaster hand wrapped in red velvet. He knelt beside me at the foot of the grave and we dug a small hole, just big enough for the box, and together we buried it, replacing the dirt and grass as carefully as we could. Then we gathered up some dust and leaves, and blew them over it, hoping any lost spirits would be able to find their way home.

We sat in silence for a long time. A couple of cats stalked the graveyard like shadows, but otherwise there was no movement anywhere around us.

"Is your mother going to tell people?" asked Angelo.

"Tell people what?"

"About what she discovered. About Alberto and Vittorio."

"I don't know. I didn't ask her."

"A lot of people will not be happy."

"That's true. Does that matter?"

"I don't know," said Angelo. "But your mother didn't mind."

"No, she almost seemed . . . relieved to know."

"My family would not be relieved to know," said Angelo.

"Secrets are strange things," I said. "They can be very exciting. But they can also be very sad."

"Which is ours?" asked Angelo.

"I don't know," I said. "Both, I guess."

Once we'd buried the hand, it felt like we'd really come to the end of something. From here there was nothing but the last few hours of dread until the actual separation took place, and it seemed like there wasn't anything left to say. I didn't know how I was going to bear it. The blue night and the quiet of the graveyard felt like the perfect reflection of my feelings. Even though the memory of our first kiss was right behind me on Keats's grave, none of that mattered right then. The whole world felt dark and threatening. Tomorrow was my last day in Rome, and the ticking bomb was louder than ever. Somehow we'd convinced ourselves we could make time stretch beyond its limits, that lying together on the blankets in our secret room, or playing all our music over again, or walking side by side, or simply being near each other meant we could exist beyond clocks and space. I thought of Alberto and Vittorio, of Dante and Giovanni, and Elijah and Isak in the film studio. Their stories, their secrets, their histories swirled around us, all these people who came before us, who seemed to prove that miracles could happen, and that love could blossom in the midst of impossible odds, even when people didn't want you to exist.

The bomb ticked, and I whispered out loud, "I can't believe tomorrow is August fifth."

"August fifth," said Angelo with a hollow voice. Then suddenly he shouted "Oh!" which startled me so much I jumped.

"What is it? What happened?"

"I can't believe I almost forgot. Tomorrow I will show you a miracle!"

"What are you talking about?"

Just then we heard someone's voice as the beam of a flashlight cut through the leaves of a thick grove of hedges. We dropped to the ground behind the grave.

"Who's there?" said someone in Italian.

There had never been a guard before, and I was terrified we'd be caught. Angelo was lying on top of me in the darkness as the beam of the flashlight swept like a scythe around the cemetery.

"I will show you a miracle on your last morning in Rome," whispered Angelo into my ear.

We shifted our heads until our lips met, and the kiss felt like a force field that would protect us from all danger, and it must have worked because soon the flashlight disappeared and the guard went away, leaving us alone.

Safe again in the moonlight, Angelo pressed himself harder against me. Removing my glasses, he kissed the side of my face, my neck, my chin, my closed eyes. I held on to his back and could feel the heat from his skin through the thin cotton of his shirt.

"If I show you a miracle," he said, "then maybe we can have a miracle of our own, and maybe all the sad secrets of the world will go away. Wouldn't that be nice?" He kissed me again, and the warmth and the sweetness were so overpowering I lost my edges, and I saw in my mind the eye of God, which was the elephant, and the oculus, and I could see the great eye as it looked down upon us, two sweating, grasping boys, lying together in a graveyard at night.

"I promise you," he said as the dirt and the grass tickled the backs of my legs. "I promise you," he said as my fingers ran through his damp, curly hair and I felt the solidity of his skull between my palms. "I promise you," he said as my chest and his chest fit into each other like puzzle pieces and our feverish bodies felt like they were going to burst into flames. "I promise you a miracle."

QUO VADIS

Even now, all these years later, I can still see everything with perfect clarity. The world was ending at 9:42 p.m., when Alitalia flight 644 would leave for New York from Rome's Fiumicino Airport.

I'd woken up with Angelo in our secret room. We usually didn't take such big risks, but we couldn't bear to say goodbye the night before. We slipped back into our clothes and I snuck back into my apartment, where I made some excuses to my mother. She was up early because flying still made her nervous. I promised I'd finish packing before the taxi came to get us that afternoon, made some more excuses, and rushed out to meet up again with Angelo, even though I was sure my mother knew exactly who I was meeting.

Angelo and I made our way down to Trastevere and had our last espressos and pastries at the little café by the fountain. We looked up toward Elijah and Jakob's balcony. We walked across the Ponte Sisto and headed to the Campo de' Fiori to buy our final paper bags of fruit. We ate everything by the stone giants in Piazza Navona. We made our way to the elephant obelisk, and I silently said goodbye to Dante and Giovanni. Then, for what felt like the thousandth time that summer, we walked into the Pantheon and stared up into the circle of sky above us, which burned white and round. We stood directly below the oculus, and felt the perfection of the dome without saying a word. The grief that radiated from us felt universal and all-encompassing, as if everyone on Earth should be feeling the same thing we were feeling, yet it was clear the rest of the city wasn't aware anything was wrong. We watched as everyone went unthinkingly on with their lives.

Angelo then led me on a walk in the direction of the train station, and soon, to my surprise, we were waiting in a long line at a huge church we hadn't visited before. Once inside, we found two seats on orange plastic chairs among hundreds of worshippers, priests, nuns, altar boys, and veiled women. Angelo wrapped his arm around my waist, and I could feel his fingertips against the flesh of my hip, gripping me tightly. Huge white marble columns lined the space on either side of us, holding up a high row of glowing windows all surrounded by shining gold and colorful mosaics. People were leaning or sitting or standing everywhere as far as I could see.

"What's going on?" I asked Angelo. "What are we doing here? I need to get back to the Monda soon to pack. My mother is—"

Angelo put his finger on my lips, quieting me. "I promised you a miracle," he said. "Just wait."

A hush came over the crowd, as if Angelo's finger had quieted everyone. I looked around but saw nothing at first. Then from behind us, a procession of people in long white cloaks entered through a side door I hadn't noticed. Some were men with tall hats; some were boys holding long staffs or tall burning candles; a few much older men had purple capes. They all moved at a stately pace to the center aisle and then turned. One of the boys swung a gold object with burning incense that smelled ancient, sweet and mysterious. It seemed to me like this same procession, with the same costumes and the same incense, had been marching down this same aisle for centuries. A kind of heavenly choir began from somewhere I couldn't see. The sound was glorious, but I was still confused. The rich smell of the incense began to make me dizzy, and I started to hallucinate as the procession disappeared ahead into the thick crowd. I knew it was impossible, but at that moment the ceiling seemed to open, and I thought I saw snow coming down. I blinked, took my glasses off for a moment, and rubbed my eyes.

The snow continued to fall.

I looked at Angelo in wonder.

"It happens every year," he whispered into my ear. "On August fifth, to commemorate the pope's dream. I can't believe I almost forgot."

Giant white flakes spiraled and fell through the air, and like so many people around me, I reached my hands upward. I discovered the snow was actually white rose petals tossed down from above, a whirling storm of flowers. I caught some and they felt velvety and soft, like Angelo's skin. The voices of the choir harmonized majestically, and a kind of joy rippled through the gathered crowd. Something was shifting, changing, and it was like everyone had become a child again. More and more hands raised themselves up toward the sky to catch something beautiful from their past.

There was one last thing I wanted to give Angelo, something I wanted him to know, but I was nervous. It felt strange to say this to him now, after the entire summer had passed. But I wanted him to know, so I leaned close and whispered my real name into his ear. At first he seemed a little confused, as if he wasn't sure what the word meant, but then it became clear to him, and a wide smile spread across his face. He raised his eyebrows as if to say *Do you want to know my name?* And I nodded.

He leaned over and whispered his real name to me, and I saw every hour we'd spent together, all the strawberries and figs, all the stories and maps, each kiss and movie and song and trembling touch. I could feel the pulse of the city and the water rushing somewhere far below, but it was our own hearts I was feeling, and our own blood that was rushing.

We looked up.

And I think to myself, when my plane takes off tonight, everything will cleave in two, history will turn into before and after, with and without, known and unknown.

But right now, right here, at this perfect moment in time, there is no luggage to pack, no taxi to call, no airplane, no secrets, no bomb, no goodbye. There is only us, as solid as the earth. Our bodies press tightly against each other, and once again we are one body.

And the rose petals are falling.

And miracles are real.

And Rome is ours, forever.

ACKNOWLEDGMENTS

In January of 2021, at the height of the pandemic, my husband, David Serlin, and I left America to live in Italy for nine months. David had won the Rome Prize, which has been given to architects, artists, musicians, writers, and academics by the American Academy in Rome for over a hundred years. Twenty-one other people were given the prize in 2021, and many of them arrived with their spouses and children, making us, in total, a community of about fifty people, living inside a very big pandemic-era "bubble." Most of the city, like most of the world, was still closed down, but we were able to walk everywhere and discover Rome in a most unusual way . . . with streets that were almost completely empty. The churches remained open, though, and since so many of them are filled with great art, we were able to visit famous paintings by Caravaggio and sculptures by Michelangelo without anyone else around.

Slowly the museums and cultural sites began to reopen, but the Italians weren't going out very much and there were no other tourists, so we could pretty much go alone to the Pantheon, the Colosseum, the Capitoline Museums, and, perhaps most extraordinarily of all, the Sistine Chapel, where we were often the only people besides the guards. I'd been to Rome before, and knew what the crowds were like—the lines, the tickets, the jostling, the yelling, the cameras, the cars. And while I was always very aware of the devastation and illness going on around us, we also felt lucky to be there. The city was quiet, and it felt, for a few moments, like it was ours. This is the Rome that opens *Run Away With Me*: the silent, empty city of a dream, one that will probably (hopefully?) never exist again. We soon became friends with the other Rome Prize winners (called "Fellows") and their families (who, like me, were "Fellow Travelers"). Most of the Fellows were working on projects that had something to do with Rome or Italy, and I often found myself in long, intriguing conversations about these projects. For instance, Katy Barkan, an architect from Los Angeles, was working on a project about obelisks, and by the end of her stay she had created a full-size obelisk from wires and mesh, positioned on its side in the courtyard of the American Academy. It was Katy who first told me that most obelisks had been built in pairs, and were only separated when the Romans sacked Egypt and pried the pairs apart. Dr. Danny Smith (whose first name I borrowed for the narrator of my book) was researching Byzantine mosaics illustrating the dreams of popes. It was Danny who brought us to Santa Maria Maggiore on our last full day in Rome—August 5—to watch the white flower petals fall from the ceiling, like snow. Danny was also the person who first took a group of us to the bottom of San Clemente, where we saw and heard the rushing water beneath the city for ourselves. I spent time alone in that room, just me and the stone walls and the sound of the water, imagining myself having fallen outside of time. Dr. Rebecca Levitan introduced us to Pasquino and the strange history of speaking statues in Rome (they're real, and there's more than one!). I'm incredibly thankful to Katy, Danny, and Rebecca for their friendship and their influences on this book.

David and I went on walking tours of the city with others from the Academy, who shared their insights and knowledge about the histories of Rome. Because we felt so isolated as a group, afloat in our great stone palazzo on the hill, we came to call ourselves "the castaways," and I want to express my gratitude here to all the castaways for their generosity and support. Thank you to the American Academy in Rome, as well, for bringing us all together and providing us with the opportunity to have so many extraordinary experiences. If you're curious what the palazzo looked like, turn again to the drawing of the Monda Museum at the beginning of the book. That, save for a few very small details, is, in real life, the Academy. David and I, and a few others, actually lived across the street in a smaller building called Villa Chiaraviglio. (My description of Danny and his mother's apartment is based very closely on the apartment David and I called home, down to the checkered floors, the heavy furniture we rearranged, the smoky walls, and the screaming parrots outside.) David's studio was in this main building and we spent a huge amount of time there sharing meals, talking, and looking out at the city from the terraces on the roof at sunset.

I would like to express special gratitude and love to my friend Deborah de Furia (after whom I named Vittorio and the de Furia Bookshop). She moved to Rome, in the country her father's family was from, after we graduated college, and was incredibly helpful in the creation of this book. She told me of her earliest memories of Rome when she first went there in high school, and the scenes with the Ciao were drawn from her memories of all the young people on those bikes whizzing by her on that first visit. For this book, she translated Dante's poem into Italian, read my whole manuscript, shared with me her incredibly helpful thoughts, and kept an eye on my drawings of Rome. She made sure everything was accurate, including the patterns of the cobblestones on the streets. I began to call her my "cobblestone whisperer," and her presence permeates these pages.

Charles Kreloff, with whom I've worked on so many of my books, told me about the two angels on the ceiling of the Santa Maria in Trivio church next to the Trevi Fountain, so I owe their presence in this book to him.

During a great conversation with Josh Siegel, the film curator at the Museum of Modern Art, he told me about Ostia, a beach town visited often by the filmmaker Pier Paolo Pasolini. Inspired by this, I created the scene where Angelo and Danny head off on their motorbike for a day by the sea.

Ursula Mitra, the senior book conservator at the New York Public Library, was generous enough to invite me to her incredible home studio, where she spent time talking to me about the work she does. She showed me the instruments of her trade (many of which I gave to Danny's mother), talked to me about the history of books and bookbinding, and told me about one of her teachers, the great Paul Banks, founder of the first book conservatory program at a university in the United States, who, amazingly, spearheaded much of the work done on the books salvaged from the great flood in Florence in 1966 (like the character I invented, Alberto Monda). Here are his seven rules of book conservancy:

- ALL BOOKS AND DOCUMENTS
  DETERIORATE OVER TIME
- THE PHYSICAL MEDIUM OF A BOOK OR
  DOCUMENT CONTAINS INFORMATION
- NO ONE CAN HAVE ACCESS TO INFORMATION
  THAT NO LONGER EXISTS
- USE CAUSES WEAR
- NO REPRODUCTION CAN CONTAIN ALL
  THE INFORMATION CONTAINED IN THE
  ORIGINAL
- AUTHENTICITY CANNOT BE RESTORED
- NO TREATMENT IS REVERSIBLE

I spent an inspiring snowy morning at the Morgan Library in New York City with Maria Fredericks, the Head Conservator there, who gave me a thorough tour of the department (which influenced some of my descriptions of the Monda Museum), and spoke to me enthusiastically about her work. She introduced me to several of her colleagues: Rebecca Pollak, Associate Paper Conservator; Elizabeth Gralton, Sherman Fairchild Fellow in Paper Conservation; Michael Caines, Senior Preparator; and Ian Umlauf, Exhibitions Preparator, each of whom generously chatted with me about their specialties. I learned so much from everyone, but perhaps the most extraordinary moment for me was when I told Maria my story centered around a mysterious seventeenth-century Italian hand-bound, hand-written book, kept in a cloth-covered box, whose author is unknown. I can't remember her exact words in response, but it *felt* as if she said something like, "Oh, perhaps you'd be interested in this book we're working on right now. It's a hand-bound, hand-written book from Italy whose author is unknown, which we keep in a cloth-covered box." It was from the sixteenth century, not the seventeenth century—but still, that's pretty close, and Maria assured me the materials, including iron gall ink, could be the same for my imaginary book. And then she got up and pulled the box off a shelf and proceeded to show me what seemed to be the very book I'd dreamed up. The main difference was that my book was filled with love poems, and this book was filled with pen-and-ink architectural drawings and floor plans of Roman buildings (including, mysteriously, an unbuilt tower designed for the Vatican by Rafael). She explained to me how the book had been bound, the materials that were used, and I took all this information and wove it directly back into my story.

Robert Williams, scholar in residence at the Newberry Library in Chicago, was great fun to email with as he shared with me his knowledge of paleography. He sent me examples of seventeenth-century handwriting (including an actual letter from Bernini), and shared with me the ways in which Danny's mother would approach the work of deciphering the love poems in the hidden book.

I'd like to extend my gratitude to the following people for their help with many aspects of my research and for their insight and support: Elliot Atlas; Zach Blumner; Cassie Brand, Curator of Rare Books, Olin Library, Washington University in St. Louis; Jean Dommermuth, painting conservator (original castaway, and host of a great podcast about the physical life of paintings called *What Is a Painting?*); Dr. Jill Gage, Curator of the Wing Collection, Newberry Library in Chicago; Dr. Yelena Gluzman, Assistant Professor of Art and Design, University of Alberta; Sara Harrison (original castaway); Dr. Sebastian Hierl, the Drue Heinz Librarian, Arthur and Janet C. Ross Library at the American Academy in Rome; Karen Karbiener, Clinical Professor, Liberal Studies and English, New York University; Rebecca Messbarger, Director of Medical Humanities and Professor of Italian Studies, Washington University in St. Louis (original castaway); Kimberly Nichols, Director of Conservation, Newberry Library in Chicago; Cathy Opie (honorary castaway); Cathy St. Germans; Dr. Christy Schirmer, Department of Classical Studies, Tulane University (original castaway); and Dr. Lindsay Sheedy, Scholar Development Advisor, National and International Scholarships Office, Purdue University (original castaway and host of another great podcast, this one on art history: *Stuff About Things*).

When I was in Rome, we went on a tour of Cinecittà Studios, and it was from the tour guide I first learned about the refugees who lived there after World War II. If you'd like to discover more, Noa Steimatsky has written some wonderful essays about this little-known part of Cinecittà history.

If I've gotten anything right regarding the factual aspects of my book, it's because of the people I've mentioned above. If I've gotten anything wrong, it's purely my own doing.

While I was working on this book, my friend Connor Jessup told me he and Sebastian Croft, both of whom are young queer actors, were starting a charitable organization to be called Queer Was Always Here. According to Connor and Bash, it will be "an ongoing project celebrating queerness throughout history, while working to build better futures for LGBTQIA+ people around the world." I was amazed at how closely that aligned with the themes and goals for *Run*

Away With Me, and if you'd like to support the organization, or find out more, please check out queerwasalwayshere.com.

Thank you to my whole Scholastic family for their ongoing love and support: Ellie Berger, Rachel Coun, Billy DiMichele, Iole Lucchese, Tracy Mack, Charisse Meloto, Leslie Owusu, David Saylor, Lizette Serrano, and Peter Warwick. And finally, grazie mille to the designer Maeve Norton, who helped bring *Run Away With Me* to life, and especially to my editor, David Levithan, who saw something in my earliest thoughts about two boys meeting one summer in Rome, and guided me with a steady hand over the cobblestone roads as the story took shape around us.

And finally, thank you to David Serlin, for everything.

BIBLIOGRAPHY

Cavafy, C.P. "He Asked About the Quality." From *The Poems of C.P. Cavafy*, translated by John Mavrogordato. London: Hogarth Press, 1951.

This poem was the inspiration for the story of Angelo and Vittorio meeting in the bookstore.

Hawthorne, Nathaniel. *The Marble Faun: or, The Romance of Monte Beni*. New York: Dell Publishing Company, 1960. First published in Boston by Ticknor and Fields, 1860.

Intervista. Directed by Federico Fellini. Academy Pictures. 1987.

Keats, John. "Ode on a Grecian Urn." In *Keats: Poems*. Edited by Peter Washington. London: Everyman's Library, 1994.

The poem was first published anonymously in *The Annals of the Fine Arts for 1819*. This is the poem with the line *"Beauty is truth, truth beauty."*

La Dolce Vita. Directed by Federico Fellini. Riama Film. 1960.

Quo Vadis. Directed by Mervyn [LeRoy]. Metro-Goldwyn-Mayer. 1951.

If you'd like to see the two boys (who I made up *before* I found them in the movie), you can see them, as described, at about the one-hour mark, in the crowd during a speech on the side of a mountain.

Roman Holiday. Directed by William Wyler. Paramount Pictures. 1953.

Steimatsky, Noa. "The Cinecittà Refugee Camp (1944–1950)." Volume 128 Postwar Italian Cinema; New Studies. Pp. 23–50. Published by MIT Press, 2009.

Wharton, Edith. *Roman Fever.* New York: Charles Scribner's Sons, 1964. The short story was first published in *Liberty Magazine*, 1851.

Williams, Heathcote. "Sacred Elephant." London: Jonathan Cape, 1989.
The first lines of this poem are: "The shape of an African elephant's ear is the shape of Africa. The shape of an Indian elephant's ear is the shape of India." This is my only intentional anachronism, since "Sacred Elephant" was published three years after my story takes place. But the observation about the ears of the elephants was so beautiful I wanted to give it to Danny anyway, as a little time-traveling gift.

ABOUT THE AUTHOR

Brian Selznick is the author and illustrator of many books for children, including *The Invention of Hugo Cabret*, which won the Caldecott Medal and was made into the Oscar-winning movie *Hugo; Wonderstruck; The Marvels; Kaleidoscope;* and *Big Tree*. With his husband, David Serlin, he wrote the beginning reader *Baby Monkey, Private Eye*. Brian has also written for the screen and stage, and his work has been translated into 35 languages. He and David split their time between Brooklyn, New York, and San Diego, California. For more about his work, visit thebrianselznick.com.